# Steampunk is Dead

The Feedback Loop BOOK TWO

Harmon Cooper

Edited by George C. Hopkins

# Chapter One

I try in vain to access my inventory list. My finger taps against thin air, waiting for my inventory list to appear. *Come on you bastard ...*

Another kick to the stomach reminds me of where I am, lying in a dirty, greasy, urine-soaked alley, watching the stars and planets whirl about in my own private planetarium and feeling genuine, full-body pain the likes of which I haven't felt in years. Blood on my lips, blood on my chin, blood on the pavement. The fight already lost, the white flag tattered.

"Come on," I say tapping my finger in the air. "Come on ... "

Another kick reminds me of how real the *real* world is, how stupid I must look trying to access my inventory list. From trouble boys and trigger men to snowed up shitbirds – the story of my life.

*Pathetic, Quantum.*

My eyes blur as I take in the man's stompers, oversized things that make him look like a toddler in his dad's sneakers.

"Ya got something else to say, ya bastid?" my assailant asks. He is East Coast to the core – that accent we've come to love and despise coupled with muscles and grease. No ducktail, but definitely slicked back. The type of palooka I shouldn't have messed with, the type of jasper who gets high off pollutes and assaults a feeble guy like me, a man with a cane. Maybe I should have opted for cyborg replacements or an exoskeletal suit. What can I say? A man has his convictions.

A kick to my thigh this time.

"C'mon – is that all you got? My sistuh hits hahduh than you! Stand up, ya pussy! Fight me like a man!"

"Leave him alone, Jimmy, he ain't shit."

*You are not in The Loop.*

The reminder has little or no effect. Still trying to access my list, still trying to choose a weapon – anything – to handle the wise guy who's kicking me like I'm a recalcitrant Harley. What I wouldn't give to access my vintage stag-handled Bowie knife – item 33 – and slice him into greaser jerky, hang his carcass up to dry. What I wouldn't give to activate my advanced abilities bar, spring into the air and land behind him and crack the back of his neck over my shoulder. Send Mr. Tough guy to the morgue before he can utter another word. Make sure the only thing he can do for the next week is eat out of a tube.

I suppose the name of the game is maim, even in the real world. Another kick and I spit blood. Real blood, my blood, no digital sap allowed.

"Youah wimpy and weak!" The man bends over and socks me in the face. "Ya heah me? *Weak!*"

*If only we could have met somewhere else…*

A final kiss from his big boot sends a sharp pain ballooning through my body. My finger comes up to access my inventory list and I hear laughter.

"Let's get out of heah, Jimmy," the man's friend says as a police siren knifes the air. "This guy's a real freak."

6

*Welcome to the real world, Quantum.*

~*~

"State your name for the record please, this Field Interview is being recorded." the police officer says. The walls of the alley strobe *red-blue-blue-red; red-blue-blue-red* with sufficient intensity to induce an epileptic seizure. I sit with my back against a dumpster, clutch my cane, and try to make sense of what's just gone down.

"Quantum Hughes," I mumble.

His pupils dilate and completely occlude the iris as he scans me – okay, this one's not human, then. No, he's part of a new Humandroid Police Program, something I would not have believed eight years ago, when I first got stuck in The Loop. There were Humandroids before I got trapped in The Loop, but they weren't as advanced as they are now. Definitely not advanced enough for law enforcement. Now here's *Homo Machina Lex Congendi Officiariis,* genuine *Mechanica Porcum Americanus* if you will, in the artificial flesh. Next it'll be ED-209s on every street corner. Who'd have thought it'd come to this? Mechanical fuzz? Goodbye civil liberties and our rapidly eroding constitutional guarantees.

"Look, RoboCop, I want to speak to a real person," I say, ignoring the pain in my jaw every time I flap my gums.

"You require medical treatment," the Humandroid tells me. "You have a fractured rib and cranio-facial injuries indicative of potential traumatic brain injury."

7

"Who are you? Dr. McCoy? Dr. Spock? Dr. Seuss? How do you know?" I ask, as the planet rotates around me.

"I've scanned your vitals twice now."

"Dammit droid, I want to speak to someone who can help me find the scum who did this to me."

"I understand, Mr. Hughes."

"Quantum, call me Quantum, and quit giving me the third degree!"

"I understand, Mr. Quantum. A human police officer is on the way. In the meantime, please tell me what happened in your own words."

"You want to know what happened?" I look up at the Humandroid. If I hadn't seen his pupils dilate, I would have assumed he was as human as me.

"Please, in detail. The video from the surveillance equipment in this alley will help us to positively identify the alleged perpetrators."

"Surveillance equipment? Wait a minute – *alleged* perpetrators?"

"Yes sir. Unless and until the individuals in question are apprehended, processed, tried, and convicted they are the *alleged* perpetrators. In accordance with the Watch Our Own People Act of 2036, surveillance equipment has been installed in all public spaces, particularly those where statistical probability indicates criminal activity is likely to transpire."

I sigh. "Listen, droid ... "

His voice goes flat and not-quite-menacing, "Mr. Hughes, my official designation is Mark9 Patrol Officer, Unit 2315. You may address me by some variation thereof. Do *not* address me as *droid* again. This is your first, last, and only warning."

"Mark9 Patrol Officer? Do you know my buddy Mark8? He and I go way back … " I say with a blood dappled grin. I've been back in the real world for nearly a month now – giving droids hell is something I've come to enjoy.

"Very humorous, Mr. Quantum. I'll be sure to recount it to the other Mark9s at the precinct who will without doubt enjoy it as much as I have. Now then Mr. Quantum, in detail, what happened?"

"All right, Marky Mark all right. So I stepped into the bar … "

"Paddy's Pub."

"Sure, whatever. Anyways, I sit down and have a beer. Then I have another beer. Then I have another, 'nother beer."

"Three beers."

"You got a calculator app, too? Listen, Ro-Man, I wasn't going over the edge with the rams or anything – got it? I was just having a few cold ones. Nothing wrong with that. This is still a free-ish country, dammit."

"Indeed sir. Is this your blood on the ground here?"

"Well, let's see, Marlowe. That's the spot I was lying in when you showed up, I'm the only one here that's bleeding. So yeah, there's a *statistical probability* that it's my blood." I can talk like a tight-ass too.

"Yes, sir. Is this your blood; please answer *yes* or *no*."

"Yes, yes – it's my blood. What, are you the Blood Police? You gonna charge me with littering for getting my blood all over this nice clean alley?

He takes a small applicator out of a pouch on his belt, delicately swabs it in the blood – *my* blood, holds the applicator in thumb and pointer finger and dilates his pupils again as he reads it."

My eyes narrow. "What's the big idea?"

The Humandroid officer flatly states, "Adjusting for your weight, stomach contents, and metabolic rate, your blood alcohol concentration in parts per million indicates you have consumed more than three beers. You are well above the legal limit, sir."

"Oh, you're frickin' *CSI Baltimore* now? Well, there's nothing wrong with that is there? I'm not operating an aeros, ground vehicle, or heavy equipment; I'm not on a hoverboard, Imperial speeder bike or unicycle. I don't even have a hayburner or nothing."

He produces a small Ziploc bag, places the swab inside, and secures the bag in his bat-utility belt. "Very well, Mr. Quantum. Do tell me what happened in Paddy's Pub."

"Okay, so maybe I had six beers. The point is, I saw these two goons across the bar looking at me funny, gowed-up on pollutes."

"Describe the men."

"Buff, slicked back hair, dangly earrings, fake tan, maybe Italian, Puerto Rican, Greek, Martian, Joey from *Friends* – who knows. I got no idea what the filth were doing here in Baltimore."

"And were they drinking?"

"Are you listening to me? They were using pollutes."

Pollutes are the name for designer inhalants dispensed by pollution masks, which were developed in the 2040s. They've become quite popular in the eight years I was marooned in The Loop, although personally I don't see what all the fuss is about. Who wants to sit around like an aardvark with a rhinovirus snuffling in designer gasses when you can marinate your brain cells in good 'ol EtOH like God intended? What the hell is wrong with people these days anyway? I'm not saying eel juice is for everyone, but it beats sitting around in neo-plague masks sucking down dope.

"So the two men were using pollutes?" the Humandroid asks.

"Do I need to spell it out for you?"

"And then what happened?"

"One of them took off his mask and asked me if I was looking at him funny."

"And how did you reply?"

"I don't remember."

"What do you remember?"

I scowled at the droid, but the change in my facial expression didn't seem to register with him. "I remember one of them asking if I'd like to take it outside. Well, I obliged, and I got one good one in with my cane before he overpowered me."

"I see. So you state that you committed the initial assault, and the subsequent physical injuries you received were a direct result of that individual acting in lawful self-defense. Does that accurately describe what happened?" he asks.

"I … wait, what?" My eyes move from the officer's perfectly sculpted face to a streetlamp in the distance. *Don't give yourself away, Quantum.*

"Does that accurately describe what happened?"

"I don't remember."

This is turning not good way too fast. I stand, wobbly, but at least I'm on my feet. Leaning my weight on my aluminum cane helps some, but not much. I'm not the biggest fan of my new walking buddy, but it's better than a wheelchair. "Look, Mark9 Patrol Officer Unit 2315, Can we just forget about the whole thing? I've got to get going."

"Do you desire to make an official statement?"

"No, I'd like to go back to my hotel."

"I'll escort you, Mr. Hughes."

"Quantum, call me Quantum."

~*~

The hotel I'm staying at in Baltimore isn't far from the gin mill, just a couple of blocks. It's an elaborate affair, with a half-donut driveway and an expansive lobby. Too much room for me; I prefer something a little cozier, something a little more disheveled, something like The Mondegreen Hotel in The Loop.

"You should receive medical attention," Mark9 Patrol Officer suggests once we arrive at the hotel. "I can summon emergency services if you desire."

I shake my head. "No meat wagons. I've seen enough sawbones over the last month to last me a lifetime. I've been poked, prodded, picked over and examined … "

"So your life chip data states," he says.

"Life chip data?" The bottom drops out of my stomach. "I didn't authorize a … a damn life chip!"

"It was likely inserted it during one of your surgical procedures, as lifechip evasion is a federal offense. The life chip allows the Federal Corporate Government to better administer to its citizens' needs. Yours indicates that you've recently had corrective spinal surgery and that you were in a digital coma for eight years."

I tap the tip of my cane against the polished marble floor. A looker walks by with a pair of getaway sticks worthy of a pinup mag. I shoot her a toothy grin and she ignores me. My thoughts return to the fact that I've been chipped like a shelter puppy – now I'm traceable, trackable, watchable and blackmailable.

*Thanks a lot, Frances Euphoria.* She's the one who signed off on my medical procedures. My fists tighten as I turn away from the droid.

"If I have a life chip," I say through gritted teeth, "why did you ask me my name back there?"

"It is standard procedure to ask a citizen their name during a field interview. It helps to establish a friendlier officer-citizen interaction. Studies have shown that an estimated–"

"Whatever, copper, I've got it from here."

I'm in the elevator a minute later, heading to my floor. Fuming doesn't begin to describe my disposition. In the past thirty minutes, I've had my ass royally handed to me and been told that there is now a CPU called a life chip installed in my head that can be used for God-knows-what. This on top of the fact that I have to give witness testimony tomorrow has my blood boiling.

As soon as I'm in my hotel room I pick up the phone and call the number Frances Euphoria gave me.

"Dammit, Frances," I say instead of hello.

"Quantum?" she chuckles to herself. "Ah that's right; you're calling on a landline. I haven't received a call on a landline in ages."

"Did you know that a life chip was installed in my head?"

"Yes," she says, yawning. "Why?"

"I told you I didn't want one! I just got my ass kicked and the droid police officer tells me all these things about me based solely on the data of my life chip. It gave me the creeps."

"Ass kicked? Are you all right?"

"I'm fine. The life chip–"

14

"Everyone in America has a life chip," she says. "It's federal law. I was planning on showing you how to use it tomorrow, after your witness testimony."

"So it's active?"

"Your life chip *is* active, but it can't connect to iNet or anything."

"iNet?" I mouth the words again. "Oh, yeah, internet inside my eyelids, the thing that everyone uses. Great, that's the last thing I need…"

"It's quite useful, much more convenient than Wi-Fi. Don't act like you haven't seen people using it before. You've been out of the recovery ward for a week now."

"I was at my dad's place; he doesn't use this shit."

"Yes, he does – everyone has one."

The thought of my dad reminded me why I was drinking at the dive bar in the first place. My mom died two weeks before I logged out of The Loop. The woman who had named me and raised me and cared for me was gone. I couldn't help but feel bitter about it. *Two weeks before I woke up.*

As Frances tells me about tomorrow's plans, my eyes settle on the Proxima VE rig set up in the room. There's an NV visor and even a reclining haptic chair.

"I have to go Frances," I say.

"Do you want me to come over or not? I'm about twenty minutes away, at the office."

"Are you sleeping there now?"

"No, I'm talking to you using nineteenth century technology now. I'm coming over, Quantum. Stay put."

"Well if you do, bring some first-aid supplies and a bottle of Jack."

~*~

I know better than to put the Neuronal Visualization Visor on. I haven't been to a Proxima World since I finally logged out, but here I am, relaxing in the haptic chair and ready to visit The Loop. As soon as the visor comes over my eyes I hear a soft dinging sound created by Brian Eno, signaling the network is ready to take me.

"What are you doing?" I ask aloud.

Of course no one answers. Who would answer?

"I'm coming Dolly, I'm coming back for you."

Dolly, the NVA Seed with whom I had a relationship with for damn near a decade – I've thought about her every day since returning to the real world, the world that just treated me to a good ol' fashioned, East Coast-style 'Welcome Back, Moron!' ass-kicking, now with thirty percent more bruises and contusions. Despite that, I'd love to somehow show her this world, to take her on a stroll through a park, hold her hand, feed some fat pigeons, catch a flick afterwards. Normal things.

Our time together comes to me in a series of flashes. Funny how memories do that. Breaking into the room next to mine to watch old movies, the hours we spent lying on my bed listening to the storm outside, the time she tried to kill me, the time she saved me, the time she morphed into something otherworldly once the Reapers arrived.

I can see her now, standing in front of me in a tight red dress, her hair in a bob, her lips crimson, chewing gum as she curls into my lap, relaxes into my grip, moves her face towards mine.

"Not real," I remind myself. "Not real." The Loop is nothing more than a glorified video game. VE equals virtual entertainment.

*Entertainment, Quantum.*

The NV Visor dings again – a reminder to log in.

Dolly's image is replaced by Morning Assassin – Aiden; the many times we killed each other and how we became friends during those last few Loop days. I see his sharp features, his dark eyes. I imagine him breaking into my hotel room here in Baltimore, imagine myself springing forward to greet him with a kick to the throat using my advanced abilities. *Yes!* My finger comes up and I access my inventory list and select a bull whip, item 201, or a stick of dynamite, item 339, or my nail gun, item 31, or my Kalashnikov, item 422.

We die together, laughing our heads off. We die together.

I realize then that I can't do it, I can't log in. I know better, I remember what happened last time; I remember what it's like being stuck and the feedback …

The feedback.

I can't imagine anything more disheartening than hearing the feedback – Satan's fingernails on a chalkboard the size of Nebraska, rabid weasels with chainsaw jaws consuming your childhood home, millions of laughing bats with vampire teeth death-spiraling behind your eyes, Stalin forcing Chernobyl reactor-melt up your nose with your Nana's antique turkey baster. The NV Visor falls to my chest. Damn the feedback.

I can't do it... not yet, anyway.

# Chapter Two

Frances knocks at my door.

"It's open."

"No it isn't," she calls from outside the door.

"Dammit."

I pull myself out of the haptic chair and make my way to the door, my trusty aluminum cane at my side. As soon as I open it Frances says, "This isn't The Loop; I can't simply kick down the ... " She takes in my appearance; her dark brown eyes fill with concern. "Geez! What happened to you?"

"Gravity experiment went awry."

"Quantum!"

"Tripped and face-planted on CementBob SquarePants."

"*Quan*-tum!"

"The spirit of Sonny Liston yet to come took umbrage at my jocose verbiage." *That one's a little closer to the truth.*

"What does that even mean?" she huffs. "Your face ... "

"Did you bring some first-aid stuff or not?" I ask, waving her concern away.

"Quantum, who did you get in a fight with? You're in no condition to go around fighting."

I shrug as I make my way to the bed. Sitting on the end of the bed sends jolts of electric fire up and down my newly repaired spine. I wince, take a deep breath. What I wouldn't give to find the shitbirds who did this to me and rub them out. There are plenty of ways to put the curse on someone: item 78, my poisonous dart gun or item 163, my baseball bat covered in rusty nails and razor-wire. The list is endless.

"You really are hopeless," she says in the kindest way possible.

Frances with her boy haircut; Frances whom I saved years ago and who returned to rescue me; Frances with her red hair in The Loop; Frances with her mutant hack – the woman has been part of my life for a long time now, whether I know how to acknowledge it or not.

Like a sister, like a mother, like a lover, she plops down next to me and immediately goes to work on my face. The proximity between us produces a strange sensation in my stomach. I'm still adjusting to human attraction, the butterflies fluttering in the tummy thing. That's not the only emotion I've found troubling in the real world – joy and regret can be equally taxing.

Frances dons a pair of non-latex hypoallergenic exam gloves, tears open a sanitizing wipe and lays it on the mouse under my eye. "Hold still. This is antiseptic and anesthetic. Just let it sit for a minute." She looks at me, shakes her head. "I can't believe you were out there fighting! You're no better than a grizzly old cat that prowls around looking for trouble."

"What can I say? Some guys were looking at me funny, or I was looking at them funny, or something. Either way, we took it outside and this is the result."

"Did you even get a hit in?"

"Of course I ... "

"It's okay," she says as she cleans me off. "It's okay if you didn't."

"I did! With my cane," I say, pointing at the damned thing. It's on the floor, lying on its side. "Look I was drunk, *am drunk*," I tell her. "I thought ... I thought I was at Barfly's in Devil's Alley. It must have been the adrenaline. I kept trying to access my inventory list."

"You have to remember that this isn't a Proxima World. There are real-life consequences here. Now you have to make a statement to the F-BIIG tomorrow looking like some fight club reject."

"Then put some makeup on me, Frances. Get me all dolled up."

"I can search on iNet for a way to conceal bruises ... "

"Thanks for reminding me!" I say, glaring at her. "I didn't want this life chip in me and now ... now ... "

She finishes cleaning my face off. "Everyone has a life chip. Get over it. FYI: most people in America don't use phones any longer, although they still exist. We–"

"We?"

"The Dream Team."

*Dream Recovery Extraction and Management* ... It's the team I formed to recover people from glitched Proxima Worlds, worlds that they can't log out from. I can barely remember those times, the early days if you will. It is even harder to believe that I formed the team with the leader of the Revenue Corporation and the Reapers, Strata Godsick. *Why has he turned criminal?* No one knows. No one.

"We use iNet to communicate. You need to be logged in to receive e-mails, et cetera from us, which is another reason that you need a life chip," she says.

"I'm still not happy about the fact that you installed a life chip without my permission. It's a violation of ... of my civil liberties!"

Frances' hands come up. "Quantum, it's *federal law*. The only reason it wasn't installed while you were in a digital coma is that you were wearing an NV Visor – removing it would have left you in an actual coma. Everyone has a life chip. They really aren't that bad."

"That's what most oppressed people say."

"Do you want me to show you how to use iNet or not?"

I give her the dirtiest look I can and she laughs.

"Is that the best you can do?"

"Yes," I say, my scowl turning into a smile.

"So, are you ready to get with the times or what?"

"Ready as I'll ever be," I say, yawning.

"Good. Most people's life chips are automatic. However, with people new to the technology, there is a manual way to turn one on. Close your eyes. I'm going to press behind your ear and you are going to see something appear on your eyelids. Once you do, move your finger and click the logon button."

"My finger?"

"There's a subcutaneous sensor in both your pointer fingers."

"They installed that too?"

"It's the best way to use iNet. There is new tech coming which allows a person to operate it without using their finger, but most people like the tactile aspect of it."

I do as instructed. Frances' hand comes to the back of my ear and a logon button appears on my eyelids, over the bridge of my nose. "Holy hell … "

I blink my eyes open. There is a subtle trace of the word still hanging in the air, likely due to my drunkenness.

"Close your eyes again and log in," she says.

"By using my finger?"

"Exactly."

"Which finger?" I ask with a grin.

"Just do it … "

My eyes shut and I drop my pointer finger onto my knee. A cursor appears. I quickly move it to the logon button and click it.

23

"We've already set up a GoogleFace message box for you. There are other apps you can use, but it is best not to rush that."

"This is almost like … "

"Yes, it is almost like accessing a list in a Proxima World. Although you can't change your appearance with this, nor can you select a weapon. *Don't forget that.*"

I open my inbox and find a general message to the Dream Team. From there I move to the upper right corner and find an internet search bar. "And it only works with my eyes closed?"

"Yes, unless you have modded eyes, which are popular but pricey. I'll send you a message now. Accept it."

*You have a message from Frances Euphoria. Accept?*

I click yes and her message appears.

Frances: Don't call me on the phone anymore. This is how you should reach me.

"How do I type back?"

"This is the crazy part," she says, "you simply *think* what you want to say and the words appear. You also have to think 'send' at the end of whatever you type. This prevents unwanted thoughts from being sent. You'll get used to it."

"How is that even possible?"

Frances: Neuroscience. Black Magic. Voodoo. I can send you links on the subject if you'd like.

Me: I'll pass. Say, what's buzzin' cuzzin?

Frances: That's your very first iNet message? 🖥

Me: It's the first thing that came to my mind. That and I want some pancakes. Can we get some damn pancakes or what? I'm starving over here.

Frances' hand drops onto mine. "Open your eyes."

I open them to find her smiling, closer to me than before. "We don't have to talk on iNet if we are together in person; however, it can be useful if we need to communicate in a tight situation."

I blink again and iNet appears. "How do I get it to stay off?"

"It fades after a few moments; you'll get used to it. You never told me how your trip to your parents" house went. How were they?"

"My mom died two weeks before I came out of my digital coma," I tell her.

"That's horrible!"

"Tell me about it … "

The room seems smaller all the sudden, darker. "I wish I could have seen her one last time."

~*~

Baltimore twinkles as we zip through the air in Frances Euphoria's aeros. It's hard to imagine that the 2050s are almost over, that in a year and a half it will be 2060. Look how far humanity has come and at the same time, how we've regressed. The new fashions, the new intoxicants, the new beings called Humandroids, the new restrictive measures such as life chips – this is us.

"Goose it, Frances," I say. "I'm starving over here."

"You and your Loop slang … "

"Old habits die hard I guess. Savvy?"

She shakes her head. "Are you ready to start tomorrow?"

"I thought I was starting on Wednesday … "

"In the morning you'll meet two F-BIIG special agents to give witness testimony about the attack in the digital coma ward. I've contacted the Dream Team's lawyer."

"No lawyers."

"What?"

"I'm not a big fan. They just want a statement, right?"

"Yes, but you should have a lawyer present anyway."

"Look, Frances, I'll give them what they want – a statement – and then they'll be on their merry little way. Easy."

"If you say so … " Her eyes dart from the vehicle gauges back to the windshield. "After you meet the agents, we'll get started on our next assignment."

A question I've been meaning to ask comes to me. "Who's our boss, exactly?"

"We are partially funded through the Department of State as well as the Digital Homeland Security Program. I suppose *they* are our bosses … "

"What about our immediate boss? Who do I report to?"

"You report to … you," she says. "Hi, Chief."

"I'm the boss?"

"You are the most experienced member of the team. We have people we answer to, but to be quite honest with you, most people in the FCG don't understand what it is we do. Hell, they still use laptops with keyboards at the White House! There's been a divide between the people who run the government and the technocrats that run the people that run the government for sixty years now, maybe longer. On one hand, we have the most advanced tech in the world; on the other hand, we still have people in high positions using the same tech my grandma used."

Light flashes across the inside of the aeros. I turn in time to see another vehicle with blacked-out windows drop into the airlane next to us. The vehicle swerves, sideswipes us. "Shit!" Frances says, losing control of the yoke. "Auto drive evasive!"

~~Automatic driving mode evasive maneuvering activated.~~

The aeros tries again. We jink out of the way and an umbrella on the dashboard rattles and bangs as it bounces off the windshield. A box filled with files bounces open in the backseat, tossing paper to the floorboard.

"Reapers?" I ask, raising my hand to access my inventory list.

Frances has both hands lightly back on the yoke, feet off the rudder pedals as the aeros maneuvers to avoid further collision. To me she says, "Strap in!"; to the aeros, "Sea Whiz Weapons Free El El!"

~Confirm Close In Weapons Systems, Weapons Free, Less Lethal.~

"What are you doing? What should I do!?"

"Watch. Strap in. *Shut up.*" A section of the rear deck splits longitudinally, folds in, and a shoulder fired weapon in a remote mount rises clear and tracks the *kamikaze*.

I glance right and see the vehicle coming in for another pass at us. We narrowly evade it; this forces us into the next airlane and throws me against the harness. My back and ribs ain't happy with this, but I'm too engaged with the action to focus on the pain.

"Be careful!"

An aerosSUV deploys airbrakes and drogue spoiler and barely drops out of our way.

"C'mon, c'mon, c'mon," Frances mutters. Our weapon tracks, locks, and fires a tremendous zombie-green *ZAP-ZAP-ZAP!*

"Ha! My AI can kick your AI's ass!" she shouts as we watch the other aero falter, stall and fall out of the sky.

"Holy Simoleons, Napoleon!"

"Confirm no other hostiles in immediate defensive bubble."

*~Confirmed.~*

Frances nods. "Sea Whiz to standby, resume manual control."

*~Close In Weapons Systems to standby, returning manual control in three, two, one – now.~*

"Jeez Louise that was intense! What in the blue-eyed world did you just do?"

She resumes flying the aeros. "Relax. I disabled their higher-function AI. That puts the vehicle in safe mode and forces them to ground and shut down. The vehicle won't restart until it has a hard reboot."

I turn – which hurts! – to get a look at her high-speed, low-drag patented aeros disabler, but it's already back in the trunk.

"I'm pretty sure that a magic green zapper wasn't available as a standard option in the 2050 models; looks like they're really offering more for your money nowadays."

Her eyes are bright, she's bouncy, still full of nervous excitement. She giggles, "Isn't it cool? They're not available in this year's models either, and I'm not really supposed to have one – nobody is – or the Metal Storm pods either. The *magic green zapper* is a *TEMP* Generator – Targeted Electromagnetic Pulse – that specifically disrupts AI. They're graytech – not supposed to exist, the whole concept violates Hindenburg's uncertainty and some of the laws of thermodynamics ... "

"Heisenberg."

" ... Huh?"

"Heisenberg, not Hindenburg."

" ... Who? Whatevs. Long story short – several of the people I rescued from a *Zompoc* World are very well connected and arranged the installation as a personal thank-you. I can even take it out of the remote mount and carry it if I need to. I like it because it's not as lethal as the Metal Storm pods. Those are ... are ... just awful. Very effective, but just awful; they put out a flying wall of depleted uranium and don't leave anything – *anything*!"

29

She shivers. I decide that I've got to get me some of that Metal Storm.

"The Feds fund us, although not very well, and not for anything like this. We have enemies in the FCG who keep trying to cut our budget – who cares about a bunch of gamers stuck in some stupid game, am I right? And Revenue Corporation buys politicians like they're on sale on EBAYmazon with free same day shipping. My point is – we sometimes meet interesting people and pick up some cool stuff every now and then, which is possibly one of the biggest perks of the job." She grins at me.

"Well, sign me up for one of those Metal Storm guns."

"Please, you hardly need something like that."

"How about for my inventory list then?" I glance out the window and watch my reflection yawn back at me. Boy, am I pooped. "There isn't a place where I can catch a little shuteye, is there? Broom closet or under a desk – just about anything will do."

"You're tired after what just happened?"

"Honestly Frances, I don't know what to think anymore. One minute I'm hungry, the next I'm ready to catch some Zs. One minute I'm getting my ass handed to me outside a bar, the next I'm whipping through the air watching you take potshots with a green laser at another aeros. Life's coming at me quick – the perfect time to rest my head."

# Chapter Three

Feedback dreams of taxis plummeting and weapons firing and bleached people screaming as explosions light up the sky. The Pier, The Badlands, Chinatown, Barfly's, Three Kings Park, my hotel. Dolly moves towards me with praying mantis arms jutting out her back holding a man in a skull mask, *a Reaper*. White hands covered in veins tug at my feet as my mom's voice screams, "Quantum, wake up! Quantum, wake up!" inside my skull.

Not gonna happen.

Feedback nightmares feedback life – life of the unholy, of the digital, of the suppressed and depressed, of the trapped and sapped, zipped and zapped. Stripped from my skin on a whim I drop into a hole in my hotel room to find Picasso, the boy with a crazed uncle. A shit-eating grin on his face reminds me of the madhouse from whence he came. The same place I feel most at home.

Inventory list. Reaper's skull, item 551. I stare at it like Hamlet, squeeze it, place it on my face. *Alas, poor Quantum, I knew him, Horatio, a fellow of infinite jest, of most excellent fancy* … The architectural layout of the room appears, displayed in a grid of blue lines. I marvel at my hand, the digital outline indicating I'm human. In the real world I'm nothing more than a crippled cynosure, hidebound by the rules of gravity and men.

*Break free.*

Running towards the window screaming at the top of my lungs is my comfort zone. My body hits the glass and I sail out, gridlines of The Loop twisting all around me, surrounded by a halo of glass, surrounded by sneering gargoyles, surrounded by the smog of the miserable city. The wind beats against my face like a pack of angry stepdads; the rain cold and unforgiving.

Don't wake up!

The desire to hit the pavement swells within me.

*Finish the job!*

My arms spread wide as I expose my neck, as my spine curves back, as my heart slams against the inside of my teeth. This is where we meet, Fate, this is where you defeat me. The big sleep imminent.

"Quantum, are you okay? Wake up!"

~*~

My eyes blur into focus, adjust to the cold light of the room. Some frou-frou melon scented candle in the corner hints at a woman's touch.

"What happened?" I ask Frances Euphoria, who is kneeling by my side.

Morning Assassin will be here any minute.

My finger comes up to access my inventory list. Start my day with war; end my day with suffering – life in The Loop.

"You can't do that here," she reminds me softly as she lowers my hand.

"Where … am I?" I ask through parched lips.

"My office … "

I look down to see my feet hanging off her couch, partially covered by a blanket.

"You were dreaming."

"Shit …" I press my palms against my eyes, hoping to rub the sleep out. "Did I say anything?"

"Dolly," she says. "You kept calling her name. You should visit sometime. She'd be happy to see you."

"I need some Joe, some grub," I say.

*When in doubt, change the subject.*

Frances is in a black uniform with a straight collar. A classy chassis, a hotbody, smoking, the bee's knees – all describe the woman in front of me. It's hard to imagine I rescued her from a Proxima World based on Arrakis when she was just sixteen. Time flies like mosquitos, sucking the life out of everything.

"The agents are in the Conference Room," she tells me. "I'll make a quick cup of coffee. For now, here's a Soylent bar."

"The dicks are here?"

"You shouldn't call them that."

"Different meaning," I say, yawning. "Well, same meaning, in my case."

33

"You need to be on best behavior," she says as she hands me a rectangular bar wrapped in plastic, "unless you want trouble."

"My middle name is Trouble," I say with a smirk.

"Shut up and eat."

"A candy bar?"

"It's not candy. It is made from soy butter, asparagus, pine nuts, coconut, spinach, raisins and fiber."

"Sounds like squirrel food."

"I practically live off these things. They'll give you energy."

I dangle the package by its tip above the floor.

"Come on, just eat it. I'll have breakfast delivered as soon as the agents leave. Deal?"

"Deal. Bacon, eggs over easy, three slices of toast, pancakes, syrup, extra butter and beer. We good here?"

"Fine, but only one beer, and a small one at that. You really shouldn't be drinking."

"Frances."

"Quantum, eat."

I sit up, wincing at the reminders of the last forty-eight hours' festivities. One look around her office tells me that the Dream Team is indeed underfunded. Everything is old, beat-up, cast-off, third hand. The metal desk is scratched and dented and rusty in spots; no two of the mismatched file cabinets are the same size or color. The desk chair was old and beat-up when I went into the dive vat; its torn vynylhyde upholstery is a mystery color that does not occur in nature. There's a makeup bag sitting on the desk, a knock off glossy as a fiend's eyes. It reminds me of the Loop; I feel right at home.

"Say, how were you able to put me up in such a swanky hotel?" I ask her. "No offense Frances, but this place would give shitholes a bad name."

"Thanks. The Federal Corporate Government has a contract with the hotel. That's how. Now eat."

"The FCG is fronting the bill? In that case, we should order some Room Service tonight!"

"Maybe." She nods at a dry cleaning bag hanging from her coatrack. "Put that on; it's your uniform. The agents are in the Conference Room, two doors down on the left. I'll brew you some coffee."

"Got it." I stuff the Soylent bar in my mouth.

"And remember to mind your manners."

"I always do," I say, speaking with my mouthful.

"One more thing," she says.

"What's that?"

"Keep last night's air rage incident to yourself, okay? We have to be careful who we speak too, at least right now."

"Why right now?" I ask.

"Just trust me. There are bigger forces in play than just the RevCo and Reapers."

~*~

"Let's get this over with."

I'm sitting across from Jake and the Fatman now, trying to work the Soylent crap out of my teeth. The Conference Room has enough room for an oval table and half-a-dozen mismatched chairs. Metal blinds separate it from the rest of the Dream Team office space. There's a diagram of an NV Visor on the wall behind the table and a single fluorescent light above us. Other than that, the room is empty.

"Mr. Hughes," the first agent says, "I'm Special Agent Reynolds and this is Special Agent O'Brian. We're with the Federal Bureau of Investigation and Intelligence Gathering."

"F-BIIGies. Got it."

Agent O'Brian is the older of the two, a fat man with a floral necktie, frayed collar, and food stains on his rumpled, two-sizes-too-small sport jacket. His cheeks are littered with pockmarks and his nose would give Rudolf a run for his money. His body showcases the cumulative effects of long hours, bad nutrition, too much booze and not enough exercise, like he's the display in the show window at WalMacy's during national *Don't Do This To Yourself* Awareness Month. If Bollywood central casting had set out to produce a compendium of every stereotypical fat, surly, burned-out, disheveled, inept, corrupt American flatfoot, Agent O'Brian would be that result down to four decimal places.

I instantly don't like him.

"Lovely. Let's see some ID, Special Agents." They roll their eyes, grunt, sigh, and work in as many other non-verbal demonstrations of annoyance and put-outed-ness as they can at the temerity of a citizen exercising his lawful right to require a law enforcement officer *not* in uniform to provide proof of identity. They take out their leather badge and ID holders, flip 'em open, flip 'em closed and put them away. I wait for them to get comfortably settled.

"Sorry, Special Agents. That was too fast. Take 'em back out, lay 'em on the table and let me get a good look at them." I wait for them to just start to bristle before I add "Please."

They repeat the whole *Theater of the Annoyed* performance as they re-dig out their IDs and lay them on the table. Agent O'Brian seethes with barely controlled fury as I read every word on his ID card *and* badge out loud, slowly and carefully, mispronouncing as many words as possible. Agent Reynolds twitches the corner of his mouth up at some inner amusement, gives me a slight nod and raise of the eyebrow as I repeat the performance with his.

"Alrighty then, Special Agents – I'm willing to concede that you're probably who you say you are. How can I help you gents?" I ask, clasping my hands together on the table.

"Are you okay?" Agent Reynolds asks. The younger of the two, probably not yet corrupt. Movie star features with green eyes, tan, buff, fit – he's in the wrong field. It's not often I use the term *handsome man*.

"Okay in terms of what?"

"In terms of your face. Have a difference of opinion with someone?"

"Slipped in the shower. Cut myself shaving. Walked into a door. Woke up on the wrong side of the bed – something like that. Now, is this what you're here about, or can we move this little affair forward?"

Agent O'Brian bites, leaning on his elbows. The veteran's eyes meet mine and he doesn't like what he sees. "We're recording now, Mr. Hughes, remember that."

"What are you recording with?" I ask just to be coy.

Of course I can see the B-drone hovering behind the two men. I tip my hat to it, and am just about to flip it the bird when O'Brian smacks his gums.

"Probably not the B-drone you're acting the fool in front of, Mr. Hughes."

Nothing like giving a couple of snoopers hell. It was something I did at least twice a week back when I was stuck in The Loop. The NPC detectives never could take a joke. The sticks up their asses were prodigious in their length and stiffness.

"Look, Mr. Hughes, we just need your statement. This can be as easy and as civil as you want to make it. How do you want it – polite and friendly or difficult and unpleasant?"

"Which would you prefer?" I ask.

Frances Euphoria enters with coffee. I blink my eyes shut and notice a red indicator flashing on my eyelids. My finger drops to my leg and I quickly scroll to the message.

Frances: Behave yourself. Breakfast will be here soon. The badge thing was a scream, though.

Me: I'm playing nice, don't worry.

Frances: Seriously, behave.

Frances sets the coffee down in front of me. "Milk, sugar?" she asks the agents.

"No thanks," grunts O'Brian. "I take it just like I like my women – hot, black, and not too sweet."

Everybody who's not him rolls their eyes.

"Black for me, please," says Reynolds.

"I'll have some cream," I tell her.

She sets the coffees down in front of us, but somehow accidentally gives O'Brian the McStarbuck's Drive-Thru treatment with his, right in his lap as he leers at her. He curses, scrapes his chair back, grabs at his crotch to get the steaming hot wet spot away from his wedding tackle.

"Oh, dear – I'm ever so sorry, how clumsy of me. I'll be right back with some paper towels." Frances gushes in patent insincerity. She never brings them.

O'Brian gingerly reclaims his seat and the agents continue once she's left. O'Brian is up to the plate again, trying his damndest to hit a homer, dampened dangly bits and all. "So you were in a dive vat when the men … "

"Reapers … "

"Reapers?" Agent O'Brian gives his younger colleague the buddy punch as he laughs. "A little early for Halloween, don't cha think?" he finally says.

"They are field agents for the Revenue Corporation," I tell him. My eyes drop to my coffee, watching the cream swirl and settle.

39

"What makes you think that?" he asks.

"Think?" I take a sip of my coffee. The cream has cooled it slightly, but it's still very hot. "I *know* they work for the Revenue Corporation. There's no thinking involved. Do a little research and you'll get the picture – Reapers work in the Proxima Galaxy for the Revenue Corporation. They're techie bastards that hit a lick off of people trapped in digital comas. They've done some vile, dirty, evil things – from imprisoning people in VE dreamworlds to coming after them in real life, like they did me. We're not talking rocket science here, fellas. Put one and two together and get three."

"The evidence we've collected indicates that the suspects were simply trying to steal NV Visors, haptic suits, any of the high-dollar VE gear from the Digital Coma Ward. Nothing we have in any way even remotely links them to the Revenue Corporation," Agent O'Brian says. "Or ... Reapers."

"You actually expect me to believe that baloney? Do *you* actually believe that?"

"I know that. We've already interviewed the suspects."

"Well if I agreed with you, we'd *both* be wrong."

"Excuse me?" Agent O'Brian asks, his jowls wobbling in irritation.

"Any more questions gents?"

Agent Reynolds asks, "You killed one of the men in self-defense, did you not?"

"No. I didn't kill anybody. The poor unfortunate tech thief got stunned and went face-down in the vat goo." I tell Mr. Junior G-man, thinking of the ponytailed button man I actually *did* drown – but I'm not going to fess that up to these schmoes. I did what I had to do; anyone with a teaspoon of sense would have done the same thing.

40

O'Brian picks up where he left off. "Unfortunately, that's where your story differs from those of the two suspects we've got in custody. They claim that you attacked them *before* they could do anything. Now it might have been self-defense at some point, but according to them, *you're* the one who started it."

I almost snort coffee out my nose, and I struggle mightily to not give them the satisfaction of seeing me do so. Their whole attitude is really starting to torque my jaws.

"Really? *Really?* Okay, I'm guessing that the F-BIIG has to have certain minimum intelligence standards, and I'm even willing to concede that the two of you probably sort-of meet them, so you *have* to be aware of just how stupid that fatuous, lame-brained, dumbass statement makes you sound. I'd been floating in that vat in Zero-G for eight years with all the bone mass loss and muscle tissue atrophy that that entails. I was so weak I couldn't even pick my ass, never mind pick a fight. I couldn't lift a finger to defend myself when that guy held *my* face under to drown *me*! So, number one: No, I didn't start anything. Number two: I didn't kill him; he was in the process of killing *me*. Number three: Tango Fox Bravo that he drowned while he was drowning me, but somehow I just can't get all boo-hoo over it."

O'Brian looks to Agent Reynolds as his nostrils flare. "No need to take that tone, Mr. Hughes. That's why we're here, so you can tell your … story."

"Not a story; that's what happened."

"What about last night?" O'Brian asks. "Who started that fight then, huh?"

"Last night? What's your angle? I thought this was about what happened in Cincinnati."

"It is, but according to the statement you gave Mark9 Patrol Officer Unit 2315 last night, *you* started the fight, *you* took the first swing. I can play it back for you if you'd like."

"Last night?"

"Yes, last night! Do you need me to refresh your memory? If you can start a fight at a bar for no apparent reason, how are we supposed to believe that you weren't the one to initiate the attack back in the digital coma ward? How?" he snarls.

He ain't the only one who's peeved. "You know, you really do put the *special* in *Special Agent,* Special Agent O'Brian. You're comparing pigs and poodles here." They both bristle at that as I take another swing from my cup of Joe. "Let me refer you to my previous statement about my physical incapacity when I woke up in the dive tank, or do you need me to refresh your memory?" I lean to the side and wave at the B-drone, "Yoo-Hoo! Heh-Lo-oh! Still recording, right? And – and my condition was well documented in my medical records. So, that dog don't hunt, you got *nothin'* Elliot Ness, drop it and move on!"

I'm standing now, way too angry to keep my seat, and I bang my cane on the floor to punctuate each point.

He stands up too. "Yeah, I see your cane," he says. "Poor crippled vat junkie. Well, don't expect any pity from me. You're like that because you choose to be that way; there are better ways to handle your condition now. A cane is a *twentieth century solution.* If you've got problems getting around, get some replacement parts."

*Breathe in, breathe out.*

"That's not what I'm getting at, agents. What I'm suggesting is this: Do you two really think a handicapped guy like me could take on those four guys? And look at what happened with the Guidos at the bar last night. I got in one swing with my cane, and then the big guy stuck it up my ass for me. You've got all the WOOPA video and Frances Euphoria's testimony. Are there any more questions or can I get to work?"

Reynolds stands, opens a small metal box, the B-drone lands in it and shuts itself down.

"We'll be back," Agent O'Brian says as Reynolds pockets the B-drone box. "We'll be back."

~*~

The blue meanies shuffle out after vowing to return. I sit, relax into the chair and slowly, carefully put my feet up on the table and my hands behind my head. My stomach grumbles, I belch and taste soy butter, asparagus, pine nuts, coconut, spinach, raisins and fiber at the back of my throat. It is not any better the second time around. A hungry goat with no taste buds might find that combination extra-yummy, but it doesn't particularly blow my skirt up.

Frances enters with a stack of stainless steel insulated take-out boxes. "Geez, Quantum, that could have gone better."

"Hey, I'm not the one that dumped coffee in Deputy Dawg's lap."

She sighs, "I'm sorry, but he was just such a racist, sexist pig. He's probably a homophobe, too, and a closet non-recycler."

"Enough about the minions of Truth, Justice and the Corporate American way. That for me?" I ask.

"It is, but first, I want to give you a quick tour of the premises. Also, how are you feeling?"

"Ravenous. No more gerbil food for me, please. It tastes like hay, algae, peat moss, and dirty socks when it repeats."

"Eeww. No, I mean about your injuries from yesterday. We should get you checked out.

"I'm here now. So give me a tour, let me eat and then we can get started with whatever it is you need from me. I won't be staying in a hotel forever, will I?"

"No, we're just waiting for the funds to put you in Government Employee Housing not far from here. It should come this week."

"Good."

I bring my feet down from the table and slowly stand, putting my weight on my cane. "It's weird ... sometimes I feel, oh what's the word? Lithe? That's it. Sometimes I feel lithe and sometimes I feel like I'm trapped in the body of an old man. It's a real dilemma."

"It's psychological. You aren't that old," she says, her hand dropping to my arm. I look from her hand to her face. Damn, Frances is beautiful and I hope there's someone out there telling her so. We make eye contact for a second longer than I'm comfortable with.

"A tour of the facilities," I say just to speak.

"Yes, follow me. You were too tired last night to look around."

We step out of the Conference Room and into a narrow hallway. On the right are Frances' office and the unisex restroom. We move left until we come into a circular room with attached offices. Six dive vats sit like sarcophagi in the center of the room, two in each row. They are much smaller than the vats back in the coma ward – no feeding tubes and no exercise gear. On the front-facing wall is a large holoscreen showing two video feeds, both monitored by a Dream Team employee.

"Are they diving?" I ask, even though I already know the answer to the question. A black man is half-submerged in a dive vat at the front of the row. Next to him is a woman with her hair tucked into a swimming cap and an NV Visor covering most of her face. The visor resembles a streamlined motorcycle helmet, a contraption that covers everything except a person's mouth and chin. Due to the fact that a person in a dive vat is partially submerged, they also use breathing apparatus.

"Zedic Woods," Frances says gesturing towards the man, "and his divemate, Sophia Wang. The man at the controls is Rocket."

"Rocket? Nice."

"Thanks. My full name is Rudraksh Vilas Paswan," he says in unaccented idiomatic Standard American English. He can't be over nineteen, Indian or Pakistani, with a lanky body and a shirt too big for his frame. On his head is a NV Visor with the optical interface flipped up. "Parents were born in India, immigrated here. I was born here hence

45

my nickname, Rocket. I discovered early that if it's more complicated than *Bubba* or *Cooter*, most Americans can't pronounce it."

"What was it again?" I ask.

"Rudraksh."

Before I can say anything, he's back at the control desk wearing his headset and typing something on a flat pane of glass with light up letters.

"What's he doing?"

"Communicating," he says.

"With whom?"

He doesn't respond.

A red light blinks on my eyelids and I open the message.

Frances: Rocket has a touch of Asperger's syndrome. He's great at his job, but if he seems impersonal, don't let it get to you.

"Duly noted," I say.

"What's that?" Rocket asks. "Sorry, just tweaking something here … "

I hear a sound that reminds me of a rabbit thumping its hind leg. I look down to see Rocket's foot tapping excitedly against the floor.

"Rocket," Frances says, "can you join us in the Conference Room? Quantum is going to eat and I want you to brief him on Steam."

"Steam?" I ask.

"The steampunk world we'll be diving to later today," Rocket says over his shoulder. "It's called Steam. Everything is … steam-y there, steampunk themed."

"Steam-y? What about my tour of the office?"

"Whaddya think you just had, big guy? This is it," Frances says.

~*~

"Steam is a VE dreamworld created by a Proxima developer named Ray Steampunk."

Rocket is eating from a package of sunflower seeds, his dark eyes wide with excitement, his foot tapping on the ground.

"Real name?" I ask with a mouthful of pancakes.

"He changed his name to Ray Steampunk in the forties, taking his named from an anime called *Steamboy*."

"Steampunk being?"

"Surely you can't be serious – you don't know what steampunk is?" Frances says.

"I am serious … and don't call me *Shirley*. So what's steampunk?"

She represses a snort. "It's a sci-fi subgenre, similar to Cyber Noir. It is noted for its usage of steam-powered things and the clothing style. Think high tech in a Victorian setting."

"The whole concept sounds stupid." Rocket says, "It doesn't make sense to me either. Why would people want to use future tech in a world that resembles the nineteenth century? But it looks cool, real cool. Confession: my ex was really into Steampunk." He licks his lips. "You two should have seen the stuff she'd wear! Hot as jalapeños, I'm telling you. Sorry, Frances."

She chuckles. "It's fine."

I glance down at my syrup-covered pancake. Only one left – I'd better savor it. Looking at the lone pancake reminds me of something.

"Frances, what about my beer? You promised."

"I promised?"

"I want a beer too." Rocket spits a shell from one of the sunflower seeds in his hand and neatly lines it up with the others on the table.

"You're too young to have a beer."

I clear my throat. "Listen you two. I'm just going to come right out with it – I don't know if I'm ready to dive yet. I've been thinking about it, hell, I tried to dive last night but couldn't do it. A beer will help."

Frances steps away from the table. "There's a six-pack in the fridge. I'll get you a beer."

"What do you mean you're not ready?" Rocket asks after she has left.

"You know what happened to me, don't you?"

"Yes, trapped in Cyber Noir. Everyone around here knows!" He spits another sunflower seed shell into his hand. "But you have to look past that."

"Well, that's rather frank."

"Who's Frank?"

"Forget about it."

"We got something big here, something huge."

"In Steam?"

"Yes," he says elatedly. "The last Proxima Developer we freed from a glitch told us about this world, and about Ray Steampunk, the developer who made Steam. He's trapped in there, you know."

"Ray is trapped in the world he created?" I ask, sawing into my last pancake.

"As far as we can tell, yes. He hasn't logged out since 2054."

"And the world is inhabited by NPCs?"

"Both NPCs and real players. It's a massive world, easily ten times the size of Cyber Noir."

"And I'm supposed to find him?"

"Yes, not just you, Frances too. It shouldn't be hard. He's the NVA Seed of the place. The God of Steam, if you will. He's everywhere, like North Korean Tourism Propaganda iNet pop-ups."

"What about you?"

"I'll be running support," he says as he empties a few more seeds into his mouth. "I've also picked up some new gear for you. Some steampunk gear. There are rules in Steam – you have to keep it world appropriate. Don't worry – I've got you covered."

"Frances said something a while back about some new mutant hacks. What's the status on those?" I ask, recalling our conversation in my hospital room.

"Almost ready."

"She said they were already ready … "

"They were … but then we ran into a slight glitch."

"We?"

"Our CWO, cyber-warfare operative. He's helping me hack and mod. Hack and mod, hack and mod … " he says, crumpling his bag of seeds.

"Well, keep me posted."

Frances returns with a beer and a half-grin.

"Anything bigger than that?" I ask, looking at the frosty bottle.

"Later," she says, "later."

~*~

I can't believe I'm doing this. In a dive vat now, my body partially submerged in the silicone substance. Frances Euphoria is in the vat next to me and Rocket is zipping around us, making sure everything is connected and that we're good to go. The oxygen mouthpiece is in place between my teeth; I bite down to secure it and breathe in rubbery tasting air.

Frances: We'll spawn together in the same place. Once we're suited up in the gear that Rocket has engineered, we can begin our search.

Me: I need another cold one.

Frances: Later.

The Brian Eno tone sounds off and I know, without a shadow of a doubt, that I'll soon be in a Proxima World. Butterflies and shit – no one can see me now, so my frown and grimace are just for sheer esthetic effect. Once more into the breach, dear friends, once more ...

"Diving now," I hear Rocket say, but his voice is thin, far away.

Colored sine waves appear on the inside of the NV Visor, increasing in speed. My eyelids start to blink rapidly and soon, they are closed and I'm feeling drowsy.

*Why are you doing this?*

No time to answer. Gravity drops and my body is suddenly floating, pulsating. I notice a strange light and I propel myself towards it.

# Chapter Four

I'm standing inside a moving train when the words appear in front of me:

*Welcome to Steam. Our records indicate that this is your first visit. You will
be in Steam's capital city, Locus, momentarily. Please take a moment to
remember some of the rules of this world:*

*1) Players using items that rely upon electricity will be penalized through their
life bars.*

*2) Shillings are used as a currency in Steam. Unlike some Proxima Worlds,
they have no real world value.*

*3) Alchemical practices are fine as long as they fit within the boundaries of the
world, which are accessible through your player dashboard.*

*4) Discriminatory comments will be logged. Repeated violations will result in
account termination.*

The rules pixilate and the train continues on.

My pants are black and crisscrossed with leather pouches, tucked into an enormous
pair of stompers. The jacket I'm wearing reminds me of something a comic-opera
admiral would wear – open lapel, a dozen golden buttons, hand stitched waist pockets.
The fingerless leather gloves on my paws are attached to gears affixed to the sides of my
wrists. I'm more yegg than man now. I'd be lying if I said I looked dapper.

"What's with the geeky duds?" I ask aloud.

Rocket: Steampunk clothing.

"You're in my head now?" I ask, looking around the train cabin. I can hear the sound of the rail wheels moving below: *cha-chuck, cha-chuck, cha-chuck.* The cylindrical lights above me make me feel like I'm in the spotlight, losing my religion.

Rocket: ¯\\_(ツ)_/¯

"Were you in Frances' head when she was in The Loop?"

Rocket: I was.

"Where is the old bearcat anyway?"

"Here, and I'm not a bearcat."

I turn to find Frances Euphoria in a tight corset inflating her airbags. The corset is attached to short sleeves, red, and lined with black lace, which form a triangle over her num-nums and from there, a taut little collar. Her getaway sticks are barely covered by a painted-on skirt with two belts draped over her thighs. A pair of Leaks sits on her head and her red hair is pulled into a ponytail.

"You designed this stuff, Rocket?"

Rocket: I did.

"You may have another career on your hands."

Rocket: I told you my ex was into steampunk.

"It looks like she was into more than that."

Frances says, "Stop staring at me and equip your gear. We'll have company soon."

53

"Gear?"

A green orb appears in front of me.

Rocket: Touch the orb, Q. It will transfer a few items to your inventory list that will help you blend in here. You don't want to go around firing a PHASR, aside from the fact it will deplete your life bar. Remember, there are both NPCs and regular players here, which means a hunting party can be formed.

"A hunting party?"

Rocket: Check out your list.

My finger comes up and finally, after a long month of recovery, I access my inventory list.

~*~

I scroll to Dolly's Seed, item 556. From there I move to a pair of enhanced binoculars, item 557. These are followed by a shoulder attachment with tube amps on the back and a forward facing gramophone horn the front, item 558.

"What the hell is this thing?"

Rocket: It's a Gramogun. Frances has one too. Attach it to your shoulder – the thing that looks like a gramophone horn is a weapon. They can shatter glass. (x)_(X)

"So can rocks."

"Gramoguns are legal here?" Frances asks.

Rocket: They run off steam.

From the Gramogun I move to a saber pistol, item 559. The grip is made of polished wood and the barrel of the gun is on the left side of the blade, pointing forward. Item 560 is a wrist gun.

Rocket: The wrist gun attaches to either side of your wrists, Q. It's good for a surprise attack.

The next item is a compass, which seems useless, and the final item is a hand mortar, item 562.

I equip the saber pistol for now and the wrist gun.

"Good to go," I tell Frances. A contraption covered in gears is attached to her left arm. Fastened to the arm piece is a shotgun with inlaid gold running along the forestock. She flexes her fingers and the gears on her arm grind to life, putting one in the chamber.

"It's electric?"

"Nothing is quite electric here," she says. "Everything is powered through kinetic energy created by steam."

"But everything here is fake; it's a dreamworld."

"Yes, but it is supposed to look as if it is powered by steam, not electricity. That's what I mean. You really don't know anything about steampunk, do you?"

"I'm not really into sci-fi," I say, admiring my saber pistol.

The door slides open and an NPC steps in. On his dome is a velvet top hat, his face covered by a mask that hangs well past his chin. Little puffs of steam spray out of two exhaust valves at the corners of his mask as he asks, "Greetings, do you have a ticket?"

"Do we need a ticket?" is my reply.

"Everyone who rides the train into Locus needs a ticket."

"Does this count as a ticket?" I ask, aiming my wrist gun at his face. "It does where I'm from."

His eyes light up. "Are you threatening me?"

"I'm asking you."

"Quantum!" Frances is at my arm now, trying to lower my weapon. I feel powerful in a Proxima World, a power I hardly possess in the real world.

I move away from Frances before she can say anything else.

Using my advanced abilities, I jab the end of my saber pistol into the NPCs chest. Steam wells out around the blade, spurts out of his nose and mouth as he falls to his knees. He grips my coat with both hands, and I give him a two hundred grain *Don't Handle The Merchandise, Buster* right between the eyes.

"Why the hell did you do that?"

"Ah, come on, he was giving us a hard time."

The NPC is now face-first on the ground, his body deflating and our train cabin filling with steam.

Rocket: You really shouldn't have done that.

"I'm the trigger man," I say aloud, "and I was just getting back into the swing of things. Have you two ever heard of shoot first, ask questions later? It feels good to … "

*… to be myself again.*

"To be an asshole?" Frances asks.

"What were we supposed to do? We didn't have a ticket … "

"All we had to do is tell him we were new players and that we spawned on the train. That's all … "

"He should have asked."

Rocket: It was a test to see what type of player you would be. There are various classes in this world, from merchant to alchemist, hunter to benevolent player.

"Well what are we?"

Frances Euphoria grabs my arm. "Thanks to you, we just joined the Marauder Class. Happy now?"

"As a clam."

"We just became a target."

"I spent *eight years* as a target," I say, trying to keep my eyes off her dairy pillows. "A few hours in a make-believe world made of steam and gears ain't nothing."

"Come on, tough guy, let's get out of here."

She pulls me towards the front of the cabin.

~*~

Frances and I are now on top of the moving train. The wind whips past our faces, makes her ponytail fly behind her like a ... well, a *ponytail.*

"We'll need to jump before we reach the main terminal," Frances shouts over the roar of the wind. "They'll be waiting for us."

There are two moons in the sky above Steam, and I can see the outline of great mountains in the distance. The sky is tinted orange and there are a few zeppelins overhead, the light from the moons curving around their great bellies. A huge cloud of black smoke heads our way from the engine of the train, obscuring and then revealing us. It even stinks of coal, which upsets my virtual stomach somewhat.

"Let's jump now."

"No, soon." She slides a pair of Leaks over the bridge of her nose. "We're too far from the city," she explains, "and there isn't an easy way to get there."

"No taxis?" I ask as I wave some of the coal smoke away.

"There are steam-powered vehicles and horse and trolley carts, but those take time. We'll want to get as close to the city as possible and then jump."

Rocket: There are other ways to travel.

"Not now," I say as I look up at the sky. A wood, canvas, and wire three-winged aircraft makes an orientation pass on us. The roar of its rotary engine dopplers in; the pilot in leather flying helmet, square-lensed Leaks and handlebar mustache paces the train, grins at us, and then gooses it and dopplers away.

"Great, Quantum," Frances says, disgust evident in her voice, "You've got the Steampunk Flying Corps on us now!"

"Don't make with the negative waves, Moriarty – maybe they're just putting the eyeball on us."

The aircraft executes a hammerhead turn and lines up on us. Flashes of fire wink atop the cowling; supersonic red bumblebees are thunking and chunking up splinters all around us before we hear the *Tat-tat-tat-tat-tat-tat-tat* of his machine gun and he zooms away behind us.

"I think we've just moved beyond eyeballing," she shouts, as she drops into a crouch.

"The Red Baron is mine!" I access my inventory and select item 69 – Dr. Quackenbush's Patented BolOcto Projector, and item 551 – Reaper Skull Mask.

The BolOcto Projector looks like the illicit love child of a trombone and a snare drum, replete with tasteful Rococo flourishes. It's all brass and silver, with a carved ivory shoulder stock and fore grip and a genuine hippo leather shoulder strap. Steam protocol is just fine with the DQP-BOP; my life bar is unaffected as it comes out of inventory. Steam protocol is not, however, as sanguine about my choice of the Reaper Mask; my life bar flashes and a warning message appears.

Her eyes narrow, she frowns at my choice of armament and glares the obvious question at me.

"I'll explain in a minute!"

Mask goes on; I shoulder the DQP-BOP. I've never had it out before, and I'm surprised when the Reaper Mask handshakes with it and provides targeting data, as my original plan had just been to spray and pray.

~*Weapon acknowledged.*~

The Red Baron comes up from behind the train at an oblique angle. His engine cuts in and out as he blips it to decrease his speed and give himself longer to shoot at us. This tactic also, however, gives me longer to shoot back. I brace up as best I can while the mask provides firing cues. The triplane opens up on us again. Compressed air blasts one-two-three projectiles clear of the muzzle. A hammer blow strikes my calf; my life bar drops to 88% as machinegun bullets thud and ping all around us.

With very subdued reports, the three projectiles burst in the triplane's path, and twenty-foot spider webs blossom like silvered silken fireworks. The shooting stops and the engine noise is suddenly gone as the whole front of the aircraft twists off and flies apart. It drops out of the sky like a stone – albeit a three-quarter ton stone moving at ninety-five miles an hour – hits the ground and explodes into a meteor of flaming wreckage.

"Whew!" I say, shooting Frances a genuine grin. "Now *that* was fun."

She points at the steam gently hissing out of my boot top. "You've been hit."

"Steam, not blood?"

"Steam *is* blood."

My life bar is down to 87% and sinking.

"I got this."

Item 13 – a big fluffy hotel towel, and my old pal item 33 ought to do the trick. I cut a pad and some long strips from the towel, Frances helps me off with the boot, holding the pad over both sides of a through-and-through bullet wound as I tie it on with the towel strips. The top of my pirate boot is just large enough to come up over bandage.

"See, just like new!" I say as the wind whips against our faces.

"What the *heck* is that thing anyway?" She nods at Dr. Quackenbush's BolOcto Projector, which now rests at my feet.

"According to Dirty Dave, it's a live capture net thrower for exotic animals and smaller dinosaurs in some of the *Safari* and *Dinosaur Park*-type worlds. The magazine contains eight canisters, and each canister contains an eight-sided bolo net woven from Sheem spider silk. The silk is practically unbreakable, so light that the big ol' net fits into a cartridge the size of a soup can. You saw what happened when the plane flew into it. BolOcto Projector."

"It's a net gun."

"It's more than a *net gun*, Frances, it's a work of art."

"Net gun."

I huff as I return the *net gun* to inventory, open my mouth to continue my clever repartee. She holds up her hand to discourage further BolOcto discussion, scans our surroundings. "Let's get off up here," she says. "According to Rocket's map, there's a market nearby. We'll be able to get you fixed up there."

~*~

Advanced abilities activated.

We jump and time becomes molasses all around us. I look over to Frances Euphoria; she's in her Leaks and there's a smile on her face that only appears when she's in a Proxima World. Everything around us is a blur, a blanket of indistinct shapes and darkened tones. We land, time speeds up and the train to Locus zips away.

"Are you going to take your Reaper mask off?" she asks me.

"Should I?"

"For now. We really don't want to bring attention to ourselves." She moves her Leaks to the top of her head. "More than we already have."

"I've never been one for rules," I say as I give her the up-and-down.

"Just take your mask off."

My mask disappears.

"Happy?"

"Rocket says that the market is just ahead. Come on."

We're ten paces away from the railroad track, near a grouping of quaint little homes connected by pipes. I can see people moving ahead, a mix of humans and NPCs. A pickup truck that looks like a cross between a Model T Ford and the Little Engine That Could puffs by. It's all flaring fenders, wood-spoked wheels, polished brass and chrome trim and elaborate decorative pin-striping. A man with a monocle drives the vehicle, puffing on a corncob pipe jutting from the corner of his mouth. His arm is similar to

Frances' – a mechanical contraption with grinding gears; the blue indicator above his head shows he's human.

He comes to a stop, throws a series of levers, cranks a hand wheel, consults a sight gauge, taps it, and the rattling engine chuffs steam and idles down. "Howdy! Where you two heading?"

"To the market," Frances says, "he's been injured."

"Want a lift?" He points down at the side runner. "I was heading there myself."

The man throws his thumb back at a stack crates behind him.

"Don't mind if I do." I step up onto the running board and catch the grab bar on the top edge of the bed. Frances mounts up on the other side.

He reverses the process of sight glass, hand wheel and levers and the engine clanks and hisses. "Hold on a moment … " He cranks a lever at the center of the steering wheel. "Just got to give her a reason to get a move on." He steps on a clutch pedal, engages the flywheel, and we're off.

"A daring young man and his jaunty jalopy if I've ever seen one," I say under my breath.

"What's that?" he asks, over all the commotion.

"Hey, you ever heard of a Ray Steampunk?" I shout. "Ray Steampunk."

Rocket: Of course he's heard of Ray Steampunk!

"Peanut Gallery," I remind our in-world monitor. "Peanut Gallery."

The driver gives me a funny look. His mustache is trimmed in a way that reminds me of a cereal box character. *Well, crunch-a-tize me, Cap'n.*

"Is this your first time in Steam?" he asks.

"You've got it."

"Yours too?"

Frances nods.

"I see. Well, Ray Steampunk is the NVA Seed," the man shouts over the clatter of the engine. "He makes the rules; he runs the place."

"Can he log out?" I ask.

"What do you mean?"

"I mean exactly what I asked – can he log out of Steam?"

"Sure, he probably can," the man says. "I don't know why you're asking me, though. It's not like someone of my social standing could ever get anywhere near Ray Steampunk."

A message from Rocket appears directly beneath my advanced abilities bar.

Rocket: I should have briefed you two more on Steam.

"Yes, you should have," I say aloud. The driver gives me a strange look over his shoulder. "I'm just going to come right out and say it – we want to meet Ray Steampunk. That's why we're here."

"Meet Ray Steampunk?" The man laughs. "Everyone wants to meet him. *Everyone.* It's pretty difficult to get into his inner circle. I've been playing this game for years, since… since about 2054, when there were only thirty thousand players. Even I have never been able to meet him. I've seen him, but he is kind of like the Wizard of Oz, if that means anything to you."

"And this is the Emerald City?"

"Hardly! We're in the outer districts of Locus, the capital city of Steam. It's more of a glorified slum."

"Designed to look this way," I remind him. My life bar blinks, reminding me of my injury.

"How many cities are there in this world?" Frances asks.

"Several dozen, but Ray Steampunk and about half the human population live in the capital."

We're at the top of a hill now, which gives us a nice view of the city on the horizon. From what I can see from this distance, Locus is heavily inspired by medieval architecture. A few zeppelins float over the city and smoke stacks jut out of every nook and cranny, filling the air with steam and smoke. The digital city rests in valley between two enormous mountains. A gigantic airship floats above the mountain on the right. It looks like a French loaf that's been sliced along its length – rounded underneath and the flat top of which is also clearly a landing strip.

"He lives in the airship above Clockpunch Mountain … " the man says. "There."

"We really need to see Ray Steampunk," I tell the driver again, 'really, *really* need to; matter of life and death need to."

"You can see him tonight on the zeppelin." The man nods at the sky. "But that's about as close as you're going to get."

"On the zeppelin?"

"Yes, he gives a nightly talk, which is broadcast by the zeppelins all around Steam."

"How does he broadcast his Fireside Chat without electricity?"

The man laughs. "You really are a newbie, aren't you?"

~*~

"The Wells Verne Market is named after some famous authors," the man shouts over his noisy retro-tech *land kraft wagen.* More people are on the street now, carrying wares with them or mingling with other players.

A woman in a *Little House on the Prairie* dress and coal scuttle bonnet shuffles in front of our vehicle clutching a leash that is attached to a spiked collar around the neck of a man decked out in a leather Gimp costume, and who has a water boiler strapped to his back, puffing out little clouds of green-tinted steam. A broad in a tight skirt stands on the side of the street with her head cocked to the left, speaking to a man dressed in the gray wool, brass buttons and gold braid of a fantasy Confederate officer, stylishly accoutered with a mechanical left leg crafted from spinning and whirring gears. I'm still getting used to the steampunk attire; the freak count is high.

66

"Airship to Imperium," a man with his head shaved and an old school necktie shouts, "from there to Victoria. Airship to Imperium, from there to Victoria!"

"Victoria?" I ask.

"It's the name for a graveyard of Lovecraftian monsters," the driver explains.

"Love who?"

"Named after H.P. Lovecraft," he says as he rumbles to a stop. He disengages the flywheel and repeats the two-handed ballet of levers and hand wheels. His engine spits, hisses, vents steam and clatters to a halt.

"Well, here we are. The Wells Verne Market."

"Thanks for the ride," Frances says as she steps down from his vehicle. "It was very kind of you."

A steam-powered traction engine rolls by, its engine chuffing and chugging, its dual exhausts coughing up little puffs of smoke. The driver's a chrome dome with a vulture's face, a parish-pick ax for a beak.

"Yeah, thanks," I tell him.

"Not a problem. There's a steam repair point to the left of the entrance. You could also visit the alchemists" section of the market, if you'd prefer that route."

"That route?"

He says, "Potions. It's good to have a few just in case you're injured and there isn't a steam repair point nearby. They've saved my life numerous times, especially in the areas outside of Imperium, near the Laputa Castle Ruins."

67

"We'll be sure to grab some," Frances says.

"I have one more question for you."

"What's that?" he asks me.

"Have you ever heard of any Reapers coming into this world?"

"Reapers?" The driver's tongue presses against the inside of his cheek.

"Yes, Reapers, from a murder guild."

"It's funny you mention that." His hand comes up to access his inventory list. Before I can react, I find myself staring down the barrel of a saber pistol.

# Chapter Five

"You're barking up the wrong tree, pal," I tell the driver with my hand behind my back. I've accessed my inventory list like this before – a quick scroll and tap. I've got my list memorized: he'll be dead before he ever gets a round off.

"Your player stats indicate that you may be Marauders," he says as he thumbs back the hammer with a *click-click-click-click.* "Asking about Reapers confirms it. On our way to the market, admin sent out a message about possible Reapers coming from the same direction you two came in from."

"You've got the wrong idea ... "

A large, official looking Federal Corporate Government *Eagle-Infinity-Dollar* logo materializes in front of Frances, overwritten with text in letters of blue neon fire:

*****WARNING! WARNING! WARNING!*****

*YOUR PLAYER ID has been logged and recorded. YOU are interfering with an on-going FEDERAL CORPORATE INVESTIGATION conducted by Dream Recovery Extraction and Management Team member ID # 0023. You are ordered to cease and desist your interference forthwith, or you may be liable for arrest, prosecution, fines not to exceed $150,000, imprisonment for up to FIVE YEARS, and PERMANENT iNet disenfranchisement.*

*****WARNING! WARNING! WARNING!*****

"A fine? Prison? *iNet disenfranchisement?*" the man lowers his weapon. "Are you serious?"

Frances smiles like a rabid shark with a chainsaw. "We are Federal Corporate Agents conducting an Official Federal Corporate Investigation; we are *not* Reapers."

You can hear her capitalize *Federal Corporate Agents* and *Official Federal Corporate Investigation.*

"In accordance with Title 867, Section 5309 US CODE, I order you to cease your interference."

The man's body shimmers, fades, dematerializes. He's gone, along with his clunky *Little Pickup Truck That Could.*

"Is that true?" I ask Frances. "Can we really do all that?"

She snorts, laughs. "No, of course not. Rocket made all of that up and did the graphic, and it works every time! If we ever do get called on it, it contains the weasel phrase *may be liable.*"

"So it's all hogwash?"

"Hogwash?"

"Horsefeathers ... "

She doesn't get it.

"Applesauce ... " I continue, "Balderdash. Bunkum. Malarkey. Ummmm ... BS."

Frances loses her confused expression. "Oh, okay, yes, it is *BS,* but it's a great, fairly unobtrusive, non-violent solution. We're in a public space, so it's better not to draw too much attention to ourselves."

One glance around and I know she's right – not many people saw our little exchange. The crowd of steampunkers is the same as it was before the man drew his weapon, freaks and geeks, fanboys and cellar-dwellers aplenty.

"I wish we could have interrogated him," I say. "I have plenty of items in my inventory list that are great for interrogating. I can work wonders with my turkey baster filled with Chernobyl reactor melt."

"A turkey baster filled with what?" Frances winces.

"You heard me."

"You really are a sick man."

"I'm simply a product of my environment."

"*Right* ... Let's get you repaired."

We advance into the market, the corners of which are anchored by small clock towers with brass gramophone horns on their roofs. True to the driver's words, the steam repair point is on the left, consisting of a giant water tank with a small, gauge-covered stand affixed to it. A few players stand around the tank with hoses connected into their forearms. I roll up the sleeve on my jacket, and sho 'nuff, there's a small entry port about the size of a dime where my basilic vein should be.

"Just plug her in?" I ask Frances.

"Just plug it in."

I take my place next to an older woman wearing a single goggle over her left eye, which is tied to her head like an eye patch. The blue lens is lined with golden spikes sticking out of the leather.

"How long does it take?" I ask Frances. My life bar lights up in my ocular display as soon as I stick the steam nozzle in my arm.

The woman with the eye patch answers, "Just a minute or so."

"Not bad."

"They have backpacks that can do this as well, called *Steam Packs,*" the woman explains. "Equip and if you're injured, just plug the nozzle in and steam up. There are modded ones as well, which constantly refill your life bar. The cheapest packs cost about two hundred shillings apiece."

"*Steam up.* I'll have to get one of those. They sell them here?"

"Yeah, over there."

I wink at Frances. "Why don't you be a doll and go buy us a couple."

"A doll?" she asks skeptically.

"What? Don't like *doll?* Would you rather be a *Generic Joe – America's Corporate Fighting Person?*"

She sticks her tongue out at me. "I think you have me confused with someone else."

The woman with the eye patch yanks the nozzle out of her arm. She returns it to the docking station and hobbles away. "You two are made for each other," she calls over her shoulder.

"Like guns 'n' ammo, huh?"

"More like oil and water." Frances reaches out and touches my cheek.

"Do I need to shave or something?" I ask.

Her hand comes back and she slaps me lightly. "That's for calling me doll."

"Noted," I tell her, watching a man crank a crowbar-sized lever at the bottom of the nearest clock tower.

"What's happening?" I ask as I finish steaming up.

"Remember what the driver told us," Frances Euphoria nods at the zeppelin above the market, "about Ray Steampunk giving a daily speech?"

"Let's see what the fat cat has to say."

~*~

Men rappel from the zeppelin, landing in the center of the market. Once they're grounded, coiled wire drops from the craft and the men connect the cables to a plug on the four clock towers. They raise their thumbs and a light flicks on inside the zeppelin.

"How's it powered?" I ask aloud.

73

With her Leaks on, Frances scans the bottom of the zeppelin. "There are people inside pedaling stationary bikes," she finally says.

"So they are creating power to … light up the inside of the zeppelin?"

"Yes, but let's not forget we are in a VE dreamworld – everything is an illusion."

"Tell me about it … "

A shadowy man appears on the side of the zeppelin's massive body. He walks towards the center of the craft, his body increasing in size as it's projected onto the side of the zeppelin. Steampunkers in the market cheer and clap.

"It's him!" someone shouts.

A crackling noise comes out of the speaker horns that surround the Wells Verne Market.

"Hello, people of Steam," the man says. "For you newcomers, allow me to welcome you most humbly to this, the best planet in the Proxima Galaxy! I am your host, Ray Steampunk, and I'm the developer of this world."

The crowd hoots and hollers, claps, whistles, and rattles their gears like they've just seen a magician pull a candy-throwing stripper out of a top hat.

"For those of you that have contacted administrators about the Boilerplate Army massing on the city limits of Morlock, know that we've dispatched a fleet of our best Air Enforcers to deal with the issue. If you wish to assist us in the defense of the realm, you can access sign-on information through the mission tab on your avatar's landing page. For today only, we've raised the enlistment bonus to two thousand shillings, but this drops back down to a thousand come tomorrow, so be sure to sign up today."

A few people in the crowd dematerialize as they access their avatar's landing page and join the war against whomever. Names have never been my forte, especially not artsy-craftsy, fancy-pantsy steampunk ones. Give me a couple of good stomping grounds like Devil's Alley, The Pier or possibly The Badlands and I'm good to go.

The silhouette of Ray Steampunk gestures like he's about to poke God in the ass. "It has come to my attention that a pair of Reapers have entered our world," he says, his pointer finger up in the air now. "For those of you unfamiliar with the Reapers, it is my unpleasant duty to enlighten you. As their name implies, Reapers are death-bringers, murderers, destroyers of souls; vile, hateful mercenaries who rape and kill and slaughter *for profit,* across the Proxima galaxy without regard to the commonly held rules of basic human decency, sportsman-like fair play, good fellowship and player solidarity. They shamelessly, mercilessly ensnare players inside a world, hold them as slaves and use them to do their foul bidding. Moreover, these Reapers indiscriminately use proscribed weapons that will kill the human player *in the real world,* a true death, a death from which there is no respawning."

Like they're reading from a script, the crowd makes the usual, stereotyped crowd noises of horrified shock and disbelief. Quivering hands are raised to mouths; wrists to foreheads. Women swoon in fright, as do some men. Players and NPCs both suspiciously eye their neighbors, rest hands upon sword hilts and holstered pistols; many, many suddenly retrieve large and powerful weapons from their inventory.

I look to Frances. "Reapers are here? Looks like Christmas came early."

She removes her goggles, scans the crowd. "Get ready to log out."

"Huh?"

Ray Steampunk continues. "For more information on Reapers, check out the bulletin post in the announcements tab of your avatar's landing page. The dastardly pair in question unmistakably identified themselves as Reapers through their base and cowardly actions. In an unprovoked attack they cruelly slew the beloved *Mister Masked Conductor Man* and without warning destroyed one of our scout aircraft. Fortunately, in his last full measure of devotion, the heroic pilot managed to far-speak his warning, and confirmed that one of them was indeed wearing a *Reaper's skull mask!* The system administrator sent an immediate all-points warning – check your inbox if you haven't already. The two Reapers are reported to be in the Wells Verne Market area, on the outskirts of Locus."

"Ah, shit."

The crowd noise picks up; friends band together, stand back-to-back. The rattle and clink of weapons nervously handled grows more pronounced. It's just a matter of time before some dumbass lets one go and precipitates a bloodbath.

"Based on their login details, we have identified them as Quantum Hughes and Frances Euphoria. I repeat, Quantum Hughes and Frances Euphoria are the two Reapers in question. Their indicators will appear red in the next few moments. Do not engage unless you are at level forty-five or higher and only do so at your own risk. For those in the market, get to a safe place or log out. Air Enforcers will be there momentarily. That's it for now. Have a wonderful evening and don't forget to join in the war against the Boilerplate Army. Until we meet again, I bid you adieu."

The light inside the zeppelin turns off.

"Ummm … "

Frances Euphoria's indicator strobes red; it's really, really noticeable.

76

"Looks like we're about to have company."

"Log out!" Her hand is in front of her now, seconds away from pressing the logout button.

"Fat chance, Frances. It's been a while since I had a true knock-down, drag out fight." Well no, I said that wrong; it's been a while since I had a true knock-down, drag out fight in which my ass was not the one getting kicked.

~*~

Frances' FCG message appears in front of her:

*****WARNING! WARNING! WARNING!*****

*YOUR PLAYER ID has been logged and recorded. YOU are interfering with an on-going FEDERAL CORPORATE INVESTIGATION conducted by Dream Recovery Extraction and Management Team member ID # 0023. You are ordered to cease and desist your interference forthwith, or you may be liable for arrest, prosecution, fines not to exceed $150,000, imprisonment for up to FIVE YEARS, and PERMANENT iNet disenfranchisement.*

*****WARNING! WARNING! WARNING!*****

A Grizzly Adams of a man snorts his disparagement and strides right through the message as he flexes his two steamed-out arms. Gears whir as an unnecessarily large Gatling gun forms on each arm.

I'm in the air before the man can plug us. My inventory list comes up and item 554 – my mutant hack ax – appears. I slice through both of his Gats and enough steam pours out of him to strip gang tags off a boxcar. He shrieks, logs out, disappears.

"Mutant hack!" Someone screams. "Mutant hack!" The crowd surrounding us thins as the faint-hearts and lightweights log out. The few steampunkers that remain all take a large step back.

My life bar glows in my display, indicating that I'm using an illegal weapon. I disregard the warning. Inspired by the saber pistol, the top barrel of my hack morphs into scimitar. *Did I tell it to do that or did it do it on its own?* No time to process the thought.

"Quantum!" Frances yells, her arm in the ready position.

"What?"

She doesn't have time to say much else.

The old woman with the eye patch from earlier springs on Frances from behind, and latches on like a backpack full of ugly. She clamps one hand over Frances' mouth, and an ugly green stain spreads outward from the point of contact.

Rocket: Alchemist! Stop her!

I aim the tip of my mutant hack at the woman. "Log out or die!"

Frances' corset spikes out like a puffer fish. The old crone leaps off in surprise, vents clouds of steam, blinks out, gone.

"Yowza! Your corset is a weapon?" I ask as a man with dreadlocks, magenta goggles, dove-gray cut-away coat and bolo tie cuts at me with a cavalry saber. I swivel to parry

78

and our blades connect; his shatter into a million pixelated pieces, and he logs out before I can make my riposte through his spleen.

This is something that will take some time getting used to – human players can log out if they're in a pickle, which strips away the satisfaction of ending someone's digital life. Sure, The Loop had yellow-bellied pink-tea bastards galore, but there was none of this logging out like a big sissy when things turned to shit.

Action-adventure worlds populated with cowards, quitters, and cry-baby whiners; what's the virtual world coming to?

Frances feels her face, which is greener than St. Patrick's Day Beer in Boston. "We need to log out before the Air Enforcers get here."

"Well you're no fun anymore – I'm just getting started!" I turn to the two steampunkers that are left and wink. Nothing wrong with a little grandstanding.

"I've been poisoned; I can't use my advanced abilities, and all of Steam thinks we're Reapers. I think that that's enough fun for one day, *don't you*?"

"Fine, fine." I aim my wrist gun at the zeppelin above the market. I fire a few shots, all of which bounce off some type of deflector shield. "A shield? I thought that kind of stuff wasn't allowed here."

"All games have their boundaries," she says.

# Chapter Six

Awake in the real world.

Feedback non-existent and my powers gone. No mutant hacks, no advanced abilities. Nothing. Just a hunk of flesh suspended in a dive vat somewhere in Baltimore. The support frame sits me up, and as soon as my face clears the tank spooge I spit the breathing apparatus out of my mouth.

I move the NV Visor off my face and keep my peepers closed. The iNet logon screen is faint, but still visible across my eyelids. I ignore it, waiting for my eyes to adjust to the brightness in the room. "Any chance we can dim the lights next time?"

My eyes come open and my head turns. Frances blurs into focus. She's in her dive bikini and covered in the gel, wet and shiny. Her arms are crossed over her chest, and she looks beautiful – tired and slimy, but still beautiful. She rubs her face where she was poisoned and her eyes meet mine. Usually she'll break eye contact first, but not this time. Her expression is inscrutable; her mouth remains a thin line.

"Well, that was not without its entertainment value!" I say to unsuccessfully lighten the mood. "If it's not too much trouble, could ya unhook these wires and tubes? I feel like Bondage Pinocchio over here."

"One second!" He's next to me in a heartbeat, tinkering away with a determined look on his face. His breath smells like peanuts.

"What now?" I ask. "We didn't exactly find Ray Steampunk."

The Dream Team monitor bites his lip. "Word will get to the Reapers that they have been identified in Steam. I expect them to start populating in the world within the day."

"Good, bring it on."

"No, ungood," Frances says, "Steam is a very conflict-themed world. Unlike the Loop which is constant Condition Orange with lots of potential individual danger, Steam is mostly Condition Yellow but with lots of organized wars and team combat and opportunities for individual combat of champions. When the Reapers come, they'll probably bring bleached people, they'll flagrantly violate the ground rules, use prohibited weapons and sow chaos and discord everywhere they go – in addition to killing or crippling real people in the real world. It's happened before. Ray Steampunk is the NVA Seed, and to prevent that, he'll unleash everything he has on the Reapers – with whom, you'll no doubt recall, we've been identified thanks to you."

She rubs her face with both hands, slicks the gel out of her hair. "Quantum, this is difficult for me to say, and I want you to know that I mean this in the nicest and least critical way possible … "

"Go on … "

" … but when we're diving, it's serious business – it's not all about you running around playing bang-bang shoot 'em up and acting the tough guy. We've got a job to do, and real people really depend on us."

"Yeah, about that … " I sigh. "Sorry if I went a little overboard."

"A little?"

She turns away and busies herself with unhooking from the vat.

"I don't get it. We're a Federal Corporate Investigative Agency, and we're Federal Agents. Can't we just contact Steampunk and talk to him? For Christ's sake, we're trying to help him!"

Rocket says, "He won't reply to any of our messages."

"Can't we log in as different people?"

Rocket twitches his head. "Not easily. Your player ID is actually more secure and harder to fake than your Social Security Number. The NVV pings your lifechip when you log in and uses that data to establish an account. Yeah, you can spoof the players some and the system a little bit, but not easily and not for long. We can change your handles, but Steampunk will know eventually."

"Why do we need him so badly again?"

Frances wipes her face with a towel. "He was the last person to talk to Strata Godsick. That's why we need him."

"So they had a conversation, what's the big deal?"

Rocket says, "According to the information we received from a different Proxima developer, Ray Steampunk was one of the last people to have contact with Godsick, before he disappeared."

"Godsick disappeared?"

"He hasn't been seen in years," Frances says.

"OK, but what about Ray Steampunk's real body. What about him?"

"He hasn't been seen in years either. He disappeared around the same time as Godsick."

"I see, so both cats are missing?"

"Exactly," Rocket says, "and it's going to be twice as hard to get to Ray Steampunk now because your identities have been released to all the Steam players. Also, they aren't cats."

"It's an expression. Okay, so we've been identified. Why don't they just ban us from logging back in?"

Rocket busies himself with other vat unhooking stuff as he says, "The Proxima Company made it so anyone could log in anywhere, as long as it's an open world. What you call The Loop was a closed world. Steam is an open world and will remain so due to anti-discrimination laws that Ray Steampunk helped create."

He helps me out of the vat and hands me my cane. The vats in the back row are empty now. I guess I'll have to meet the other team members another day.

"The shower is in that room," Frances says. "Once you're cleaned off, I'll take you back to your hotel."

"Will you stick around for a while? I wouldn't mind some company, or a Hawaiian pizza for that matter."

"I'd love some pizza!" Rocket says.

"Sorry kid, this is a private party."

"We'll see," she says with a soft smile. "Go get cleaned up."

~*~

"Goose it, Frances, I'm starved."

Aeros whip past us as the afternoon sun reflects off their hoods. My mind is still filled with images from Steam, from our brief combat to the general feel of the place. It's been a while since I've been this excited, damn near giddy. I feel like I'm in my own skin again.

"You know, you really do cause a lot of trouble," she says, her eyes trained on the airlane. "We could have been undercover in Steam, but you had to go and kill the train conductor, gun down the airplane and that was *before* the incident at the market. You're like a bull in a china shop!"

"I could be a bomb in a china shop … "

Frances glances to me. "Just be more careful next time. Is that too much to ask?"

"Jeez Louise, you're making me feel like the bad guy here."

"I'm just saying, Quantum. While the Dream Team may not have much authority in Proxima Worlds, we do have a code of ethics to uphold. Namely – don't be an asshole."

The word stings and I let Frances know that I'm upset through a long bout of silence. She drops into a lower airlane and we press past a mother driving an aeros while singing along with her children. Her lips move as she sings along, somehow reminding me of my own mother. We exist because of our mothers, and it is amazing how quickly some of them are forgotten. The reared become the rearing and the cycle continues. Seeing the children in the backseat makes me wonder if I'll ever have a younger model. Probably not.

"What are you thinking about?" Frances asks.

"Ankle-biters."

"What?"

"Kids."

She laughs. "Why, do you want some?"

"I don't know. I don't think I'd be a good dad."

"You'd be a great dad," she says. "If you learned to behave yourself."

"You think so?"

"As long as you taught them to think before they acted." Frances sticks her tongue out.

"That's the problem with our world sometimes – too much thinking and not enough action. Samurai made their decisions in the space of seven breaths."

She nods. "And how did that work out for them?"

~*~

The pizza delivery Humandroid is waiting for us as soon as we arrive at the hotel. Frances pays and I take the piping hot cardboard box from the droid. I can practically taste the cheese as we shuffle into the elevator. It takes every ounce of self-control I have not to drop the box onto the ground and devour the pie like a little piggy.

"Beer," I say as soon as Frances opens the door to my room. "I'll call Room Service."

"No need to call them – you have iNet."

"I'm too hungry to deal with that damned contraption."

"Don't worry. I'll take care of it," she says, sitting on my bed.

I'm next to her in a flash, peeling open the pizza box. Real food. Real chunks of sugary pineapples and melted cheese and hunks of Canadian bacon and crumbles of crispy bacon – I haven't salivated this much in ages. I'm practically soaking my shirt with drool.

"It's … so … good … " I say with my mouthful. The slice is down moments later and I'm working on round two, stuffing it in my mouth like they stopped making pizza yesterday.

"Slow down," she laughs. "You'll get an FDA Monitor if you're not careful."

"I haven't had pizza in …" I stop chewing.

"Eight years?"

"Bingo. I should have eaten some after I came out of my coma, but I just … there were so many other things I wanted to eat."

A knock at the door indicates the beer has arrived. From my vantage point I can see Frances talking to the concierge, who is clearly a Humandroid evident in the stiff way he carries himself. She returns to the bed.

"You ordered some forties? That's what I'm talking about! You sure are catching on."

She smirks. "You know, you really don't deserve a treat, but I'm proud of you today for going back to a Proxima World. That took a lot of guts."

"Guts are something I've always had a lot of," I say as I drum my hands against my belly.

The caps come off and we clink the large beer bottles together. The beer – real beer! – has a way of settling my nerves, filling me with warmth. It is a shit beer, as are most beers that come in forty-ounce bottles, but it is still better than digital beer, the type I routinely drank for breakfast at Barfly's for two subjective years.

Frances moves closer to me. "Want to watch something on TV?" she asks.

"Do they have any old detective movies?"

She leans over me to get the remote. "I'm sure we can order something."

~*~

*~I have a terrible, terrible confession to make. That story I told you yesterday was just a story.*

"Frances?"

*~Oh that? Well we didn't exactly believe your story.*

*The Maltese Falcon* continues playing on the holoscreen. There are three finished forties on the floor now and one half-finished soldier on the nightstand. Frances Euphoria is next to me, her head resting on my chest. I start to move her off.

"What is it?"

Her hand comes to my cheek.

"I thought you were sleeping … "

I glance back to *The Maltese Falcon*. Black and white – if only things were that simple.

"Look at me, Quantum," she says, her eyes slightly unfocussed. "Dammit, look at me."

"What's come over you?" I ask.

"Just a little drunk." She hiccups and covers her mouth, smiles. "I can't … don't normally drink a forty. I don't normally *hic* drink anything, at least in the real world."

"You nearly drank two," I tell her, just to say something. I'm feeling the effects of the alcohol too – nothing like being drunk in the real world, especially after nearly a decade of fake hooch.

Her hand comes to the back of my neck.

*~Do they have to know about me? I mean, can't you shield me so I don't have to answer their questions?*

"This movie is boring, Quantum." She slaps my cheek playfully, laughs. "B-double-O-Ring!"

88

"This is a classic!"

Dolly and I watched the very same flick countless times. The developers of The Loop uploaded hundreds of classic detective movies to the in-game TV network. *The Maltese Falcon* was by far my favorite. Dolly's too. Damn, we must have watched it a hundred times.

Frances Euphoria presses her body into mine, breathing heavily.

"What's the big idea?"

She kisses me before I can say anything else. With my arm wrapped around the small of her back, I bring her in for another kiss. My skin is tingling now, my heart thumping against the inside of my chest.

"I'm drunk, Quantum," she says, her lips inches away from mine. "I'm drunk."

"Welcome to the club."

She pushes away, presses her back against the backboard of the bed. "Sorry," she says, her face turning beet red.

"Sorry for what? For the kiss?"

Frances nods, her eyes dropping to the blanket. "We shouldn't ... I shouldn't ... "

"I got no problem with it. Life's too short to ..." I lose my train of thought and pull her closer to me.

"You know *hic* why we can't ... " She pushes me away.

"We're only human," I tell her.

"I should go." She rolls to the corner of the bed and tries to stand.

"Damn, Frances you're drunk as a skunk, loose as a goose, soused as a louse!"

"Ha! What are you … saying … " She collapses back onto the bed. "I may need to stay here," she finally whispers.

"That's fine by me. I can sleep on the haptic chair, if you'd like." My eyes dart from the drunken vixen to the chair on the opposite side of the room.

"You can sleep in the bed with me," she says as she lies back down. Her legs splay open and she pulls her knees up. Frances sways her knees back and forth, turns her head towards me. "Kiss me again, Quantum, kiss me again. Sleep in the bed *hic* with me … "

"Hold your horses … "

I'm already on my feet; the alcohol giving me newfound strength. I probably should be using my cane, but then again, I probably should be doing a lot of things. I'm in the haptic chair moments later, cursing myself for not going back to the bed with Frances. How often do opportunities like this arise?

"Kiss me, Quantum." She tries to sit, but collapses again. "No, stay there. Stay away … "

"You sure are a lightweight, Frances."

The light on the NV Visor flickers in the corner of my eye. I could log in to The Loop right now. I could visit Dolly and we could finish *The Maltese Falcon* and go on a killing spree together in The Pier. We could go to Barfly's, we could take a stroll through Three Kings Park, we could …

We could …

~*~

Morning a bullet to the brain – awake to die again. My mouth is dry and my head plangent. I open my heavy lids to find Frances Euphoria sitting on the corner of the bed, her head in her hands. There is enough light coming into the room to make me want to murdalize the sun.

"Hangover?" I ask, my mouth dry as the Atacama. The shit beer has taken its toll as all shit beers do.

She doesn't make eye contact with me. "I ordered some Hangover Over."

"Which is?"

"You'll see … "

There's a single knock at the door. Frances drops to her feet, wincing with each step she takes towards the door. The concierge hands her a plastic bag and she delicately steps her way over to me.

"Drink one," she says, reaching into the bag. Her face is puffy, her short hair shooting left from the way she slept.

"Does this crud actually work?" I take the Hangover Over can from her and examine it. It has a comical picture of a drunken man getting kicked in the ass by a giant boot.

Frances Euphoria pops the top and chugs it down. She blinks rapidly, her face brightening. "Like a charm," she says as she tosses the finished can back in the plastic sack. "Humans have spent a lot of money figuring out ways to make hangovers go away," she yawns, smiles an uncertain smile. "This is the best of the best. Drink yours and we'll go. I'll order breakfast to the office. Also, about last night … "

"Yes?"

Her eyes narrow. "It never happened, got it?"

Sometimes I'm slow on the uptake; this isn't one of those times. "*What* never happened?"

She nods, satisfied.

"What about our clothes?"

"An EBAYmazon drone should be here any minute. Go take a shower and I'll set your new clothes in the bathroom."

# Chapter Seven

Breakfast burritos wrapped in foil sit on a Styrofoam plate in the Conference Room. I'm opening the first one before I can sit down, not even taking the time to add salsa to it. The new clothes Frances Euphoria orders me aren't half bad – a black collared shirt and black jeans with a hole torn at the knee just to be stylish. Torn jeans are in style again, as are jeans with multiple designer brands screen-printed across them, proceeds to benefit the on-going Syrian *immigrant* crisis. Fashion – kill me now.

"Slow down, Quantum," Frances Euphoria says. "You'll choke."

I try to say something, but my mouth is too stuffed with tortilla, eggs and bacon to make anything but a series of animal sounds. Rocket is at the other end of the table, sipping from a cup of McStarbucks coffee. His hair is disheveled and his eyes bulging, rimmed by dark circles. In front of him is a bag of cashews.

"No sleep last night?" I ask him.

"No," he says, "I was working on our little problem. What about you?"

I glance to Frances and she frowns. "What kind of problems were you working on?" I ask him.

"Reapers have shown up in Steam," he says. "I was there last night; I heard about them."

"You were in Steam?" Frances asks. "You weren't authorized for that."

"I had to figure out a way to change the color of your player indicator. People will attack you if they see the red color."

"Won't they see our names?"

"That's an easy fix; I've already hacked into your character profiles and changed your handles. Of course, if they do more than a cursory scan, they'll be able to uncover your player ID. However, I don't think anyone will do this."

"What are our new names?" I ask.

"Steamboy_889 and Steamgirl_889."

I reach for another burrito. Damn, it feels good to taste Mexican food.

"And what about the color of the player indicators?" Frances asks.

"I fixed those too." He sets his cup down, goes for the nuts.

"How?"

"Alchemy. I found an Alchemist Alley in Locus and did some asking around. As soon as you log in, you'll need to drink the vial of pink liquid I give you. This will change the color of your player indicator from red to green."

"So people will think we are NPCs?" I ask with my mouthful.

"Yes!"

"That's brilliant," Frances says. "People won't look twice if we're NPCs. They definitely won't do an in-depth scan or anything."

"You can thank me later," Rocket says as he tosses a handful of cashews into his mouth.

~*~

The dive vat. The oxygen mouthpiece is between my teeth, the NV Visor on my head. I'm in a vat next to Frances, both of us in Dream Team dive gear. Above me is an ArachnaMed SpiderDoc, something I hadn't seen in here before. I suppose this was a worst case scenario installation, but it still reminds me of the fact that this isn't all a game, and that immediate medical intervention may be necessary. I guess all jobs have their ups and downs.

"I'm going to have you populate in the center of Locus," Rocket says. "Remember to drink the vial as soon as you arrive."

The Brian Eno tone sounds off. I'm suspended now, floating as colored sine waves race across the inside of my NV Visor. The speed increases and I feel a drowsiness coming on. A pulsating light appears in the center of my forehead and I hurl my body towards it.

~*~

The player indicator potion appears in front of me and I add it to my inventory list. Hello item 563. One chug later and I'm good to go.

"Why are the dames so much hotter than the guys in Steam?" I ask. My indicator is green now. To anyone asking I'm just a lowly NPC.

Frances laughs. "What do you mean?"

Rocket: I changed your costumes, Q.

"Got it, Rocket," I say aloud, "but my point remains: why are the broads so much hotter than the guys?"

Frances Euphoria and I are in a makeshift bazaar situated around a giant fountain with clockwork cherubs astride mechanical dolphins, spraying mist into the air. Her skirt is low-slung and dark violet, long in back, short in front, trimmed in black lace. Black leather garters secure thigh-high black and white striped stockings; pointed, side button shoes with studs and gears encase her tootsies. Her ta-tas spill over the top of the tightly laced, hooded corset of the same shade and material like foam in a pilsner glass. Black and white sleevelets that end in fingerless gloves cover her arms. Around her throat she wears a white and salmon cameo on a black velvet ribbon, and a miniature bowler with two pheasant feathers perches atop her head. And of course, Leaks disguised as the ubiquitous heavy welding goggles. She's always been a choice bit of calico, the jammiest bit of jams. In her new get-up she's surpassed the cat's meow, upgrading to the kitty's roar.

I glance down at my own outfit – a striped overcoat with an ornately tooled leather shoulder rig on top of the jacket; a black leather cummerbund with sewn in loops and topped off by little rivets; black pants tucked into ankle high boots with embroidered stars on their sides. Nothing about this outfit makes sense.

"Don't worry, you look cool," Frances says. True to Rocket's hack, her handle reads Steamgirl_889. She squeezes her fingers together and the gears on her arm whir to life. The shotgun barrel lifts out of her arm and returns to its not-so-subtle docking station.

"Cool? Are you still drunk?"

"I kind of like Steam Quantum better than Loop Quantum."

"Keep it up, Frances."

Rocket: Would you like a mask?

"No, Atlas, I don't want a mask. I just want … I want to look like a guy who means business. Not a guy on his way to a gothic Halloween party."

Rocket: Okay, no cummerbund next time.

I equip my wrist gun, item 560, which attaches itself to the gear on my right wrist. The sound of gears shifting indicates that it's ready. Aiming my arm in front of me, I fire a pretend shot at a smokestack in the distance. The two moons sitting in the air behind the smokestack gets me wondering. "Is it always night here?"

"It's always *dusk* here," Frances says. "Everything in this world is about the mood, the setting. It's only light enough to cast some shadows."

"And it's like this everywhere?"

Rocket: Actually, Frances is wrong. It's only like this around Locus.

I point at the airship floating over one of the mountains on the outskirts of the city. Planes like wood and canvas dragonflies move to and from the airship. Enormous pipes, big enough to be visible from where we stand protrude from the mountain, fill the air with thick clouds of steam which roll over the city like an ominous mist. "So we need to get up there?"

"That's where Ray Steampunk is," Frances says.

Rocket: I asked around last night. You need to get to the airship and from there, to his inner chamber. He is said to have enormous Steam Enforcers protecting him – be ready for anything.

~*~

Air bleeds from crossover ducts that weave in and out of the buildings surrounding the streets and large temperature gauges alternate on the street corners. Frances Euphoria and I pass Victorian clothing shops, gear repairmen and a guy hawking top hats. A vehicle rattles by, its engine exposed and its pistons pumping up and down, releasing hot air with each movement. A haymaker if I ever saw one. It's followed by a steam-powered motorcycle, coughing up exhaust like a lifelong two pack-a-dayer.

"Reapers are here! Reapers are here!" A boy in a cream shirt tucked into a pair of trousers shouts into a cone. He's on a crate in front of a newspaper stand, wearing a bowler hat with goggles resting on its brim. "Read all about it – Reapers are here!"

"They sell newspapers in Steam?"

Frances nods. "Everything here is done for a reason – to enhance the experience of the end user."

"I'll take one," I tell the little twerp.

98

"One shilling, please," he says.

"Frances?" I ask.

She opens a little pouch on her belt and retrieves a coin.

"This is so strange," I say as I crack open the paper. "I've never read a newspaper in a digital world before. There's just something ... wrong about it."

"I finished the entire *Dune* series *and* the knock-offs *and* the fanfic when I was trapped in Arrakis. Twice."

"How meta," I tell her as I scan the headlines. "Ah, here we are." I turn the paper to Frances, showing her our sepia-toned, woodcut-style portraiture from yesterday. "It's a good thing I was wearing the skull mask. You, on the other hand ... "

Frances' hair changes from red to blonde. "Better?"

The newspaper boy points to the sky and I follow his finger to something moving through the air.

"What is it?" I ask.

He looks at me incredulously. "You've never seen that before?"

"No," I say, "We are ... new NPCs. Just generated."

The little crumbsnatcher gives me a funny look. "They're Air Enforcers."

An explosion about a hundred meters away rumbles the ground. With my advanced abilities bar activated, the world moves like molasses around me and I aim my wrist gun in the direction of the explosion. I hold off firing when I see a pair of Reapers rip through the explosion riding steam-powered motorcycles.

Reapers – their bodies clad in Lee Mouton road warrior leather and fantasy Viking wear, their muscles inflated, their masks deformed skulls. I'm just about to fire at them when Frances grabs my firing arm and jolts me out of advanced abilities.

"What?" I ask, catching my balance. "The Reapers are getting away!" My finger comes up so I can equip my mutant hack.

*"Quantum!"* Frances kicks my feet out from under me and lands on top of me just as an Air Enforcer sails over us, his canvas wings spread wide as he controls his craft through joysticks attached to his harness. He's followed by three more Enforcers, two male and one female. They wear matching leather aviator helmets with flaps that extend over their ears; their eyes are covered by goggles; the blue indicators show they're human. Their slipstream scatters the newspapers into the air; the newsboy cries out in dismay and chagrin. Puffs of steam trail behind the Air Enforcers as they continue their pursuit.

"We need to get in on this!" I say, on my feet again.

"More are coming!" the newsboy shouts. He leaps up and pulls down a slatted wooden covering for his newspaper kiosk. He's gone in a flash, logged out.

A squadron of Air Enforcers zips over us, causing a small tornado.

"This way!" Frances says, squeezing my hand tightly. Her blonde ponytail is lashing against her face, her skirt billows against her admittedly shapely legs as she leads me through the windstorm caused by the Air Enforcers.

Her shoulder hits a large wooden door. We tumble in, followed by shrapnel-like debris and loose newspapers. I slam the door shut behind me and fall onto my rump, laughing.

"That was crazy," I say, my back to the door.

"Excuse me," the shop owner says curtly, "I trust that the two of you are prepared to make a purchase after that rather boorish entrance."

~*~

My next question comes naturally. "You don't happen to have an Air Enforcer set-up, do you? Something to fly with?"

I stand, dust off my striped jacket and make sure everything is in working order. Frances does the same, straightens her skirt and adjusts her boobage. A black cat curves through my legs, making very un-catlike chicken clucking noises.

"Why would an NPC want Air Enforcer gear?" the shop owner asks with a twinkle in his eyes. He has a tremendous Billy F. Gibbons white beard that goes all the way down to his stomach, and is stylishly curled at the ends. He wears a red frock coat over a pearl gray vest. The golden watch chain is a nice touch; shows that he pays attention to detail.

"Who doesn't want to fly around and see the sights?" I ask.

The cat rubs around my ankles and clucks like a chicken some more. I reach down and run my fingers through its silky coat, which it seems to like.

"Aha! You're using a potion to mask your player indicators!" the shop owner says. "This makes me wonder if your names really are Steamboy_889 and Steamgirl_889, which, to not put too fine a point on it, are pretty darn stupid and solidly lacking in the originality department."

Rocket: They're not *that* stupid.

"Look, pal…" I say as the gears whir on my wrist gun.

"Quantum!"

"Cool it, Frances." I keep my firing arm aimed at the shop owner.

"A short fuse this one has," the shop owner says, chuckling. "Now see here, Quick-Draw, I don't care if you're masking your identity or not – that's your business, I couldn't be less interested. However, you barge into my shop the way you just did – you buy something. That strikes me as a relatively simple and straight-forward business proposition; does it strike you that way as well? Or do you perhaps require some convincing?"

The man taps his toe on the floor, and I hear the sound of grinding machinery as a panel above and behind him slides open to reveal a cannon-sized barrel, pointing directly at us.

"Nice one, Quantum," says Steamgirl_889, "way to make friends and influence people."

"Allow me to showcase my patented *Efficacious Exothermic Enthalaptic Equilibriator.* It will freeze you solid faster than a fish can fart!" says the proprietor. "Does sir wish a first-hand demonstration of its efficiency?"

"Freeze solid? How's that even possible?"

Rocket: It's possible because of steam…

"Now's not a good time, Big R."

"I await your definitive answer," he prompts, as he twists the end of his white beard. "Inquiring minds want to know."

I look to Frances. "No. Don't need a demonstration. You?"

A rime of frost forms at the muzzle of the freeze-cannon, slowly creeping its way rearward.

She shakes her head. "I'm good. Frozen solid is pretty darned unpleasant, especially transmitted through an NV Visor."

"All right, all right," I say. I put up my wrist gun and reach for the sky. "We'll buy something."

"Excellent!" The shop owner claps his hands and the ice cannon returns to its docking port in the ceiling. He is around the counter moments later, a grin writ large across his phizog.

"What do you sell, exactly?" Frances asks.

"What do I sell *exactly*?" he laughs. "I sell the things that dreams are made of; I sell exactly what a pair of Marauders like the two of you need!"

"We aren't Marauders," I tell him.

"Yes we are," Frances says under her breath.

The man moves past us now, beckoning us forward. "Of course you're not Marauders; how presumptuous of me to have thought so. Right this way, right this way!"

He stops at the corner of the room in front of a series of polished brass speaking tubes that could have come from the bridge of the *Britannic*. He selects one, flips open its cover and shouts, "Visitors! We have visitors! Lower us to basement two, Chacho! *Pronto!*"

A voice comes out of a pipe affixed to the ceiling. "I'm sleeping … "

"You can't be sleeping if you're speaking to me, Chacho! Wakey-wakey, hands off snakey! I don't pay you to sleep!"

"Pay? Ha!"

"Come, come," the shop owner says as Frances and I approach him cautiously. "Good, stand right there. And you stand right there, my fine young miss." He points at a circular platform about nine feet across. The cat hops on the platform and he picks it up, hugs it, rubs his cheek against its head. "There's my good puss. I know you think that it's just right for cats, but I'm afraid you can't come, Chicken," he says.

"The cat's name is Chicken?" I ask.

He grins. "You've heard how she communicates – one couldn't very well yclept her with a moniker like *Flipper* or *Tralfalz*".

Rocket: Why would he want to clip her with a harmonica?

"Now's not good, Peanut Gallery."

Chaco's voice comes from the ceiling, "Good to go."

"All aboard!" The bearded shop owner places the cat on the floor, just outside the platform. "Ready?" he asks us.

"Do we have a choice?"

104

"Why certainly my good fellow, there's always a choice!" he says with a disarming grin and a cheerful tone. "You can continue your passive-aggressive bullshit, in which case I'll freeze you solid and display you outside as a particularly festive snow homunculus, or you can keep your festering gob closed and avail yourself of my services."

"The latter will be just fine," Frances says for me.

The circular platforms drops, leaving the ground floor of the shop behind. The light fades as we descend and Frances' hand hooks around my arm.

"Ah, yes!" our ailurophiliac host exclaims as the platform comes to a stop. "Here we are, my charming young lovebirds!"

One glance up and I see Chicken the cat's eyes reflecting in the half-light as she peers down at us.

~*~

The three of us stand in front of an enormous wooden door. Two lanterns are attached to the wall above the door, their lights flickering across the darkened corridor. Marking the entrance are two prickly cactuses in pots that read *Le Jardin,* which seem a little out of place.

"Not-Marauders like the two of you always need some extra gear to keep the upstanding forces of truth, justice, and the Ray Steampunk way off your tails!"

"Do you usually sell to both sides?" I ask.

105

The shop owner laughs. "Sides? Here there are no *sides*, gentle sir, only customers. I purvey to all who wish to buy; to those discerning hoplophiles who can afford and appreciate the exquisite quality of my wares. I recognize no gods, bow to no master, espouse no cause whatsoever save that of sheer, unadulterated commerce. That said, of course I don't friggin' advertise the fact that I do sell to not-Marauders such as yourselves; no sense in stirring up the hoi-polloi unnecessarily, both here or in the world up there. It's better this way all around, I find."

He knocks twice on the door, hesitates, lowers his hand. "Oh bother, what is the code … ? One moment while I ask Chacho." He turns to a conveniently located speaking tube, puts two fingers in his mouth, produces a piercing whistle and yells, "Password!"

"*We Will Rock You,*" comes the reply. "Now quit bothering me. I'm trying to rest."

"Ah, yes!"

The merchant of disaster returns to the door and starts up. *Boom-boom clap! Boom-boom clap!* The booms made with his fist and the claps made with an open palm. A locking mechanism sounds and the door pops open.

"Here we are!" He takes a deep sniff of the room, as if he's inhaling its essence.

The room is mahoosive, practically a cathedral underground. Hanging from the walls is a vast assortment of steam-based weapons. In the center of the room is a massive exoskeleton suit, easily eighteen or twenty feet tall. It reminds me of the Comsuits the American Military has started using in Iraq back in the real world. I naturally make my way over to it.

"This is… steam-powered?" I ask, running my hand along a piston on the back of its knee.

106

"Correct! The Steamsuit EXO 76, based on the Andromeda model used in the real world but, of course, Proxima World specific. They were banned about a year ago."

"Does it work?"

I look up at the thing and see the mounting ladder for the operator. The pilot's seat is button-tufted Corinthian leather; the waldo controllers are brass and ivory, teak and polished aluminum. It's beautifully cared for, cleaned and detailed like a 1957 Chevy Bel Air Nomad at the Museum of Classic Detroit Iron. Not bad, not bad at all.

"Alas, that would be in direct contravention of the latest updates to the *Official Steam Laws of Armed Conflict,* handed down from on high, so to speak, by our wise, just, and benevolent NVA Seed," he says as he runs his hand through his beard. "I purchased this after the most recent war from a gentleman from Babbage Town who was also not a Marauder, and only took it out to pillage and murder on Sundays."

I notice that he doesn't actually say *no.*

"The last war?" Frances asks. She's standing with her hands behind her back, polite as ever.

"The War of Northern Aggression, my pulchritudinous young non-Marauder, but don't spare it another thought; the foes are vanquished, the honors distributed. The world looks just the same, and history ain't changed – or something. Anyway, weapons and gear." He turns to the wall. "Now ... where is it?"

The shop owner stomps his foot, which gets some gears cranking beneath him. The floor rises, allowing the bearded man to travel to the top of his weapon cache, leaving Frances and myself about nine feet beneath him. "Here it is!" he calls down to us, his hands cupped around his mouth.

I give Frances a funny look and she laughs. "Just play along, unless you want to wind up as Quantum-cicle."

"Roger that."

The shop owner moves around collecting his things. He mumbles to himself, runs through some math equations aloud and claps his hands together, making a show of whatever it is he is doing. Soon his platform descends.

"The first thing both of you need are Steam Packs. You," he says, waving me forward. "Put this on, tough guy."

He tosses me a backpack, leather, with a metal canister attached by buckles to its body.

"It's a piston engine," he explains, before I can ask. "The intake port is there, the exhaust port there. Air comes in and steam is produced. Exhaust exits from the pipe at the bottom of the pack. Attach the tube to the port on your arm." My hand comes to my shoulder and I find a retractable cable. Stringing it down along my arm, I stick the nozzle in the correct port. The backpack vibrates and my life bar comes alive. "Will this keep me from dying?" I ask.

"No, but it will keep your health status at an optimum level. For milady," he says, turning to Frances, "I have the same thing, but slightly smaller and more feminine, suggestive even."

He hands her a shoulder pack with a strap that goes across her chest. She attaches the cable to her arm and the pistons start up on her back, making a sound which resembles a muffled typewriter.

108

Rocket: Looks good, Frances!

"The next thing the two of you need are some upgraded weapons! Speak softly and carry a big stick – the bigger the better!"

"What's wrong with my wrist gun?" I ask, looking down at it. It's not the most powerful thing I've owned in a dreamworld, but it's definitely handy.

"That little thing?" He frowns like a petulant Chrismahanukwanzivus bringer of toys. "*That's* the best you can do? A big, bad, rough, tough, smack-talking not-Marauder like you? Ha! My doo-dad is bigger than that!"

"It's not that bad."

"Pfft! Watch and learn, Young Padawan." He brandishes a serrated sword with a five-inch shotgun barrel attached to the handle. "Add a little *boom* to your stab." Like a martial arts master, he demonstrates how one would theoretically use the sword and fire the weapon. "Say one opponent is here, and the other one is on your other side. You cut right and turn your wrist back, aiming the barrel in the other direction. Two birds with one stone. It's delightful!"

"It's not bad … "

"I call it the Slice Bang."

"Thank you, sensei," I say as I take the weapon from him. The handle is gilded, adorned with the unnecessary curlicue and filigree embellishments that seem to permeate Steam. Still, it is killer-diller. A few practice swipes later and I'm ready to shiv some Reapers.

"For the lady, a shoulder pad with an attached steam missile aka a Shoulder Rocket. It loops under your arm here and sits right over your shoulder, like this." He waves Frances forward and attaches it to her. "Hook this portion into the gears on your left arm … "

Gears crank on Frances' arms, accepting the enhancement.

"That's ridiculous … "

"No, it is *world appropriate*. You won't be breaking the rules by using this. You *will* be breaking the rules if you whip out an RPG. Where there's a will, there's a way; and where there's a way, there's a buyer." The shop owner makes the universal sign for money by rubbing his thumb and two fingers together. "Now then, my tooled up *kameraden*: from the lofty twin peaks of shooterationism and slashatization … " he casts an appreciative look at Frances' décolletage … "to the more mundane but still not-too-shabby depths of compensatory remuneration."

"The shakedown," I say, looking to Frances. "How much will this stuff cost us?"

He looks at me, shakes his head, sighs. "My young friend, if I may be as so bold as to offer some free friendly advice? As difficult as it may be for you to believe, there are those who might find your constant carping, and dare I say it – *pissing and moaning* – just the slightest bit tedious, and in fact take umbrage at your unrelenting and unwarranted denigration of goods and services of undeniable quality, so much so, in point of fact that they would be sore tempted to put their pointy-toed size fourteen and a half elf slippers so far up your ass that you'd be tasting shoe leather for a month. Not, of course, that I would ever count myself amongst that number, but I can certainly see how some might be disposed to feel that way."

Frances snickers. I give her the *it wasn't me* face.

110

Beardy continues, "I must say, however, that as charming and salubrious as I find your company to be, circumstances require me to affix the customary fifteen per cent PUWYB surcharge to your bill."

~*~

We leave the shop broke as a joke. The Steam Pack stays on and the Slice Bang goes into my inventory list, item 565. I'm itching to use it, but the time will come and it'll be there, waiting for me. The Shoulder Rocket perches on Frances Euphoria's shoulder like a pirate's avian accomplice, ready to blow something to smithereens.

Frances reads the bill as we walk, and suddenly guffaws, "Oh this is great! The fifteen per cent PUWYB surcharge? *Putting Up With Your Bullshit!* That's so *funny.*"

"Yeah, a genuine hoot-fest," I grumble.

Rocket: Select the compass I gave you and follow the yellow line.

Item 561 comes up and a broken yellow line appears in my display. It cuts north, left at the next alley.

Rocket: The line leads to the entry point for Ray Steampunk's airship. From there, you're on your own. By foot, it will take you at least an hour. You can cut this time by running at your top speeds, which will deplete your life bars – world rules. Your new Steam Packs will keep your life bars full, so problem solved. Remember, Steam is an *obstacle-free world*, which means you can run without worrying about hitting something.

"Why didn't you tell us about this earlier?" I ask.

111

Rocket: You didn't have Steam Packs.

"Why didn't you give us Steam Packs?"

Rocket: I spent most of the initial budget on clothing and other gear.

"It's fine … " Frances Euphoria arches an eyebrow at me. I get the urge to pull her into my arms and I stuff it back down – not here, not anywhere.

"You ready?" I drop down and stretch, just to get a rise out of Frances. "Who do you think is faster, you or me?"

"See you there."

Everything blurs as we sprint at our top speed, the broken yellow compass line beckons us onward. Bursts of light and color fill my peripheral vision; the terrain blue shifts as I approach and red shifts as it recedes behind me. Frances is clearly visible out in front, her arms moving rapidly, her skirt and ponytail flying behind her, her hat still securely perched at a jaunty angle, pheasant feathers whipping in her slipstream. I increase my speed, pull up alongside her; she laughs over her shoulder, puts her head down, zooms away from me, vanishes in the distance. I'm going as fast as I can go – I don't have any more. I follow the yellow brick road and enjoy the sensation of surrealistic super speed.

Lightning streaks, life of the Flash. My world is distortion, a smudge of impressions that make no sense at my current pace. Wind resistance non-existent, I exist in a vacuum held together by a broken yellow line, a suture separating my new false reality from the false reality I already exist in. Laughter comes and I let it spill from my lips; for humanity, for the fact I'm doing what I'm doing in the world in which I'm doing it – this to be interpreted in any way it seems fit.

I am the signal of a neuron travelling down an axon, gapping synaptic gaps, synapsing, releasing chemical messengers, triggering electric charges, dispersing to the other sectors of the brain, returning before the message can be processed.

My first name almost makes sense at this speed. My last name doesn't do me justice.

~*~

We slow and the world slows with us. Faces come into view, the clinks and clangs of the city of Locus hits my ears. Metal meets metal, twists metal, boils water, releases steam, moves pistons, hisses air, toots and leaks oil. The attention to detail here is stunning.

"Want to race back?" I ask Frances. Nothing like a little grandstanding to reset the mood.

"You want to lose again?"

"Ouch."

We're at the base of Clockpunch Mountain now. A man hawks tickets in front of a cable car filled with people.

"Say mister, you gonna buy a ticket or what?"

One glance down and I see a small fry in an orange-checked sack coat and a little red bowtie. He's got a lollipop in his mouth, but the way he rolls it around reminds me of Winston Churchill.

113

"Come on, Jules," a woman in a white top hat says. Her dress is skintight and lacy. Draped around her neck is a fox fur with the head still attached, with beady little eyes that follow me.

"Your kid?" I say as she passes.

"Have a problem with that, mister?" the little twerp asks.

My hand comes up to access my inventory list and Frances pulls it down. "Remember, we're NPCs," she says as they pass. Besides, there's no telling what the actual relationship is there. The woman could be a Brazilian man and the kid could be a lonely barista in Brooklyn.

"Or it really could be her kid … "

"That's possible too. Some parents spend more time with their children in Proxima Worlds than they do the real world. A recent study showed that … "

"I get it Frances," I say, winking at her. A number flips down above the ticket booth, advertising that there are only six seats left. "We'd better hurry."

We approach the window to find an NPC steam-robot, if that's what it could be called, selling tickets. His entire body is made of cranking gears and there is a huge mustache on his face, reminiscent of Mr. Potato Head.

"Two tickets," Frances says.

I hear a compression sound as the robot springs to life, mechanically taking a ticket from a stack and slipping it through the slot separating us. He does this operation again, and it is at this point that I realize he doesn't have legs – only a torso.

"Four shillings," the robot says. "Eight shillings if you would like a souvenir."

"What type of souvenir?" I ask.

His head turns to me, awkward and stiff. "A postcard of your photograph in front of Mr. Steampunk's gate mailed to your home in the real world."

"We don't need that," Frances says.

"Okay," I tell the robot, "one pass with the souvenir postcard and one without."

Frances laughs to herself as we make our way to the cable car platform.

"What's buzzin' cuzzin?" I ask with a grin. A digital fog has settled, making it difficult to see the two moons that always sit over Steam.

"A postcard?"

"I want to remember what you look like in your steampunk gear."

"Stop it," she says, pushing me playfully.

"A picture is worth a thousand words, right?"

Rocket: I have plenty of pictures of Frances and you in your steampunk gear. I can forward them to you if you'd like.

"I'll stick with the postcard."

# Chapter Eight

We reach the top of Clockpunch Mountain and file out.

"Three minutes until the next departure!" The conductor shouts. The cable car to Ray Steampunk's airship is something else entirely. The passenger compartment is a weird amalgam of classic San Francisco cable car and 1950s Greyhound bus with touches of Dr. Seuss, replete with teak and mahogany structural elements, brass and chrome fitments, and the obligatory garishly gilded golden gew-gaws, curlicues and filigrees. It sits on a frame, the rear end of which tapers upward into an Eiffel-esque open work support arm with dual pulleys that ride on the overhead cable.

The motive engine is especially surrealistic, even for a fantasy dreamworld. At the front of the frame is a large ovoid brass pressure tank that's decorated like a Fabergé Easter egg, only gaudier. From this protrudes an enormous pair of metallic chicken legs, complete with scaly toes and claws. The pressure egg with legs sits astride a unicycle mounted in another openwork support arm; the chicken feet curl around the pedals and firmly grip them. A painted and pinstriped chain runs from around the unicycle flywheel to drive trolley atop the cable.

The conductor pulls over a large, ornate clutch lever and sets the catch. As he connects a hose from the steam tower to the Easter egg tank the legs begin pedaling, the flywheel rotates the chain, and all kinds of unnecessary gears in the drive trolley hum and whir.

116

"Pretty, isn't it?" Frances asks, her eyes reflecting the city below.

Locus boasts numerous ornate smokestacks; there are airships of all descriptions in the air above the city. Buildings that resemble the homes of nineteenth century Russian oligarchs are lit by enormous gas mantle lanterns. In the distance, a structure houses a giant engine with spider-like ducts that sink into the earth. Clock towers of all sizes tick-tock in a way that would drive Captain Hook mad – Steam is otherworldly, an amalgamation of a present and a past which never existed until now, the digital future.

"It has its charm, but it's nothing like my old stomping grounds."

I recall the layout of The Loop, from The Mondegreen Hotel to Devil's Alley, from The Pier to The Badlands – there's no place like home, said Ms. Gale, and maybe she was right.

"All aboard!"

I hustle to the front of the cable car, hoping to get a view of the airship as we approach it. We haven't really discussed what we'll do once we get there, and I have a feeling that simply asking to speak to Ray Steampunk won't do the trick. Fat Cats behind mahogany desks aren't usually the most accessible people in *any* world – real or VE.

The stop-gate drops into its slot, the conductor lets out the clutch and the cable car jolts forward. The large metal chicken legs drive the unicycle flywheel and we move steadily towards the airship. I laugh – I can't help myself; a gaudy brass Easter egg with metallic chicken legs pedaling a rococo fantasy cable car up to the *Graf Zeppelin's* ultra-big brother is the second-craziest thing I've ever seen.

People decked out in steampunk garb point and chatter and exclaim all around us; every single passenger is accessorized with some kind of heavy welding or aviator

117

goggles and not one of them is wearing them. As you'd expect, their conversations are Steam specific, ranging from Reapers, to the best place to buy a steamcycle, to the battles taking place in Morlock against the Boilerplate Army. I catch the lil' half pint from earlier, sitting in his lady's lap, necking, and playing international appendages – *Roman Hands and Russian Fingers.* I guess he probably really isn't a kid after all. In a different world I'd toss him out the window, use him for target practice.

Frances squeezes my hand. "You ready?"

"For what?" I ask.

"Well, we may have to … break our cover to get close to Ray Steampunk."

"I have no problem with that," I say, thinking of my Slice Bang.

An ornate speaking tube in the corner of the cable car crackles into life:

*~Your attention please! Your attention please! Reapers have been reported in the vicinity of the airship! Logout or prepare to defend yourself! Logout or prepare to defend yourself!~*

Too late.

~*~

The rear end of the cable car explodes in a cloud of digital shrapnel and debris. Injured players trail plumes of steam as they spill out of the gaping rent like M&Ms dumped from a king-sized bag. The quicker players log out before they plunge to their

118

virtual deaths; the stunned and injured splatter like algorithmic bugs on a digital windshield as they hit the ground below. I rapidly equip my Slice Bang and prepare to activate my advanced abilities bar when two Reapers sporting steam-powered jetpacks surge into the open cabin, pumping the air full of bullets.

Frances pushes me out of the way, yells "Clear behind!" and in a whir of cogs and gears fires her Shoulder Rocket.

The rocket connects with the closest Reaper and blows her into an expanding cone of pink mist. I activate my advanced abilities and run through the air, slashing the second Reaper's bullets down and away with my Slice Bang. I land on him, jam the blade up and in and trigger the shotgun.

He blows out of the cable car with a hole in his torso you could heave a Chihuahua through. His head catches on the jagged metal, and he pinwheels away. A ball of flame blasts through the center of the cabin, buckles the frame, twists the car body, and separates me from Frances.

"Frances!" I run, kick off an upholstered bench and sail into the growing gap.

"Ha! Gotcha!" She grabs the straps of my outside-the-coat shoulder holster rig and drags me in.

"Incoming, eight o' clock low!" she yells and points. Time to quit fooling around and drag out *los shooters grandes*; I equip the Reaper's skull mask, item 551 and mutant hack ax, item 554. It spreads up my arm, forming a gun with a muzzle the size of a basketball.

The targeting reticle locks on the two jetpack equipped Reapers zooming up on us. My life bar blinks; it's taking a beating, but my Steam Pack keeps the bar in check.

I zap the first one into drifting pixels before he can get any closer. My life bar dips, recovers somewhat as the Steam Pack chugs to keep up.

"Quantum, DUCK!"

A steam rocket skims over me, and the second Reaper, a big, busty, Rumple Minze-looking piece of work pops like a napalm filled zit, but not before she gets off a very definitely non-Steam approved RPG of her own. Flying glass and shards of wood and metal blast through the cab and smash the rear cable arm. The whole cab lurches, tilts, and Frances and I toboggan towards the wide open. The drive trolley, Easter egg pressure tank, crazy pedaling chicken legs and front support arm are still attached to the main cable and carry on business as usual.

The muzzle of the hack gun jams up against one of the few remaining benches, and the spirit of Super Dave channels me as I wrap the non-hack arm around Frances and fire the weapon. The blast launches us back up the slope, past the NPC conductor who's wrapped his arms around the clutch lever and up onto the top of the Easter egg tank. The cab and frame disintegrate; all that's left are the drive trolley, tank, still pedaling legs and Frances and me.

The muzzle of the hack gun has belled into an Elmer Fudd blunderbuss, and it *hurts*! My vision is red-tinged and the hack ax and Reaper mask won't go back into inventory. I finally check my life bar.

"Holy Crap, Frances! I'm almost dead!" My Steam Pack is chugging for all it's worth, but I'm still almost dead. She turns to me, eyes wide, concern writ large on her face. She pulls the tube from her arm and piggybacks it into my Pack; hers kicks into overdrive and my life bar creeps upwards.

120

"No – what's yours like?"

"Shut up," she says. "I'm okay. You need to *not* die."

We sit there side-by-side. Ornate, elaborate, pointy and uncomfortable Easter egg embellishments dig into our butts as the mechanical chicken legs pedal us inexorably closer to Ray Steampunk's Eagles" Nest.

~*~

The magic pedaling chicken legs settle into their docking point, vent steam and cease their motion. My health bar finally came back up enough for me to return my two big no-no items back to inventory before anyone notices – I hope. NPCs are move all around us as they secure the contraption, solicitously help us down, and pester us to make a statement about *the incident*. We're at the corner of an airstrip on top of Ray Steampunk's craft. From what I can tell, the runways are laid out like the flight deck on a Nixon Class aircraft carrier – an elongated "X" to allow aircraft to launch and recover at the same time. The entrance to Steampunk's crib – a gothic revival style castle – is separated from the public areas of the strip by a massive stone and iron barbican, guarded by two enormous armored figures.

"Quantum, your player indicator is flashing red!"

"What?" I turn back to Frances. I wave my hands over my head, as if I can swat it away like an annoying insect. "Wait a minute … yours is too!"

"Potion!" she says, and we both slam one down.

No effect.

"Crap! Our login info comes up with our real names too," says Frances.

"Oh, we are so screwed!"

A boiler-suited NPC confirms my prophetic assessment when he glances our way, does a Warner Brothers double-take, sprints to a speaking tube and screams "REAPERS! REAPERS ON THE LANDING STAGE! REAPERS ON THE LANDING STAGE!"

He draws an enormous revolver and I ventilate him before he more than half-turns towards us. An air raid siren overrides all other sound; players and NPCs alike panic and scatter.

"Quantum!" Frances shouts, forcing my wrist gun down.

"There comes a time in a man's life when he has to play the role assigned to him. Let's move!" I shout back.

I hop down from the landing stage and Frances follows.

"We really shouldn't – "

I grab her arm, pull her down and cover her with my body. A steam missile narrowly misses us and sails into the Easter egg water tank; it ruptures like an enormous brass water balloon, and my life bar takes a big hit when it showers us with boiling water and sharp flying metal. My vision tinges red again, and I can't access my inventory – again. My Steam Pack chugs and races, and I watch my life bar crawl upward.

At least a hundred green-coated NPC soldiers of Ray Steampunk's Household Guard, in bearskin shakos and with bayonets fixed approach us in firing line formation. They roll forward no fewer than three Gatling guns and a brass cannon, in beautiful parade ground order.

My life bar hits nominal, continues to climb, and I'm in the game again.

"Frances," I shout over the migraine inducing air raid siren. "He must be watching us; he's got to be! Ray Steampunk, I mean."

"You think?"

"There's Reapers right in his front yard – hell yeah he's watching! Equip your mutant hack and let's take care of business. Maybe we can lure the head honcho out of his shell."

~*~

We jump for them as a wall of flame and flying metal erupts from the guardsmen; the landing stage behind us disintegrates in a cloud of wood and metal splinters. The seemingly indestructible pedaling chicken legs are perforated and blow over the edge of the airship. Then we're in amongst them, and it's frog-in-a-blender time!

For NPCs, these guys are good; they don't break and they don't run despite the fearful slaughter we're inflicting on them. They're disciplined and professional; as fast as we kill one, it seems like two more step up and try to get the bayonet in. Frances and I stand back-to-back and our Steam Packs clank together as we move.

More soldiers swarm in from who knows where, and Frances alternates barrels as she fires her hack gun to clear them away from her. In her non-hack hand she's got a wooden stocked submachine gun with an odd-looking snail drum magazine sticking out of the side, and she uses that to clean up the ones the hack gun doesn't get. She's holding up her end, but her heart doesn't seem to be in it, somehow.

On the other hand, this is where I lived for two subjective years; this is what I do; this … this is who I am. I never feel more alive than when I am become death, destroyer of worlds. Unleash a killer in a foolish world with petty rules and watch the destruction he wreaks; unleash a man once chained and fueled solely by violence into a world damn-near dainty as Disneyland and let the carnage unfold. I am slaughter incarnate; I am death on two legs.

These guys keep coming; we are reaping them like rice, and yet they come on. Usually, when any group of NPC combatants takes significant casualties they'll attempt to disengage, conduct a fighting withdrawal, or break and run, depending on who they are.

I've never seen them keep coming like these guys do; never even heard of it.

They suddenly break off their assault; the surviving NPCs back away from us, weapons still leveled. One catches my eye, grins, and gives me the two finger salute; the rest hoot and jeer at us. I see their eyes look up and track something behind me. I jump and roll.

A fist the size of a garbage aeros smashes down in the spot I just vacated; it leaves a crater that would make a nice pond for steam powered mechanical geese. The ground thunders and shakes; the five story armored statues are not just imposing decorations.

Rocket: Steam Enforcers!

"We need to go! We need to go NOW! LOG OUT!" Frances screams.

"I'll take the one on the left," I say as I blast it with my hack gun; my show of force blows the dust off it, but that's about it. The Steam Enforcer lifts its foot to give me the pancake treatment and my hack morphs into the battle ax blade. I dodge, swing at its supporting leg. Golden blade meets shiny silver ankle, bounces off, no effect – not even sparks. Stomping foot lands; the Enforcer pivots, bends, and backhands me across the field. The blow crushes my Steam Pack and knocks my life bar down a good chunk; I'm still in the fight, but now there's no magic first-aid.

"QUANTUM! We. Need. To. Go!" Screams Frances, even as she charges the second Giant Decepticon of Doom with guns a-blazin'. It stomps her flat and grinds her out like she's some high-heeled, leather clad cigarette butt.

"Frances!" I say, scrambling to me feet.

Rocket: She's okay; she's here – Now LOG OUT OR DIE!

"No! *Bullshit*! Nobody kills my friends! I'm not going anywhere until I get me a piece of those big bastards!"

With my hack ax at my side, I sprint at the Frances crusher. It leans down to meet my charge and flicks me away like I'm an inconsequential booger. The scenery whirls around me in an inner ear disturbing blur of color and motion. I thump into something solid and feel the stars, the planets, the tweety birds circling around my head.

*That's* going to leave a mark in the morning, and now my life bar is so far down that if I sneeze wrong I won't be able to access inventory or use my weapons.

Rage fills me, washes over me and through me. Life bar be damned! I am invincible; I am unkillable; I am ten feet tall and bulletproof with my hair on fire! The hack ax encases my arm and morphs into a tremendous, disproportionate serrated blade. I pick myself up and go for Big Bastard Number One.

*Focus your anger. Do it. Channel all your energy into the blade.*

The voice comes and I don't recognize it.

Rocket: NOW! LOG OUT NOW!

*Focus! Do it!*

Great! *More* voices in my head now.

I ignore the voices. As I run, I equip the suicide bomber jacket, item 300, and replace my mutant hack with a stick of dynamite – item 339 – and a twenty liter can of gasoline, item 117.

My inventory list disappears and I grin at the two towering mechanisms. *Nedelin Disaster Time!*

# Chapter Nine

Awake in the real world, stuck in a vat. The slight ringing in my ears subsides, but the shit-eating grin on my face remains. There is nothing like a suicide to set the record straight in a Proxima World. Sometimes the only way to get the best of your enemies is to take them with you.

I spit the mouthpiece out. "Get this shit off me, Rocket."

"Working on it, Quantum."

I can hear him tinkering with Frances' dive vat. The support frame sits me half up and as I disconnect the NV Visor, I'm instantly blinded by the light in the room. "We really, really need to change the lighting in here … "

I blink my eyes shut and the iNet login screen appears and fades away. The urge to rip myself from the vat comes and I suppress it. Rocket is hovering over me now, his breath reeking. He could use a shower too, but I suppose we all could.

"Why does it feel like we were in there for a couple of days? That always gets me." The support frame sits me fully up and I twist my neck around, listening for that satisfying crack.

"The same reason dreams seem to last forever or disappear in a few seconds," he says as he deals with some cables and tubes.

My eyes adjust to the light and I look over to Frances, still sitting in her dive vat with her eyes closed.

"You all right?" I ask.

"All right ... enough," she finally says.

"It was just a battle," I say. "We can't die, you know."

"I know but ... " She bites her bottom lip. "We don't have a lot going for us in Steam."

"What do you mean? I thought we did pretty well today."

Rocket says, "There are Reapers there now and surely they know about you two. Why else would they attack the cable car? Both of you have also been ... blacklisted, and the indicator potion doesn't seem to work on the airship."

"When the going gets tough, the tough get bigger guns. We can handle it. If you two didn't see, I gave those Steam Enforcers a parting gift courtesy of The Loop.

"Which didn't do anything," Rocket says. "Remember, I'm monitoring your actions. I saw you explode and guess what the Steam Enforcers did? They went right back to their perches."

"No effect whatsoever?"

"Nope."

"Drat."

Frances shakes her head at me. "This is serious, Quantum. We need to get to Ray Steampunk. We need to talk to him and it is going to be even harder to reach him now."

"We'll figure something out."

"Also," Rocket says, "those F-BIIG agents stopped by again, the ones from yesterday. I told them to come by again tomorrow morning. They didn't seem too happy about it."

"I'll do everything I can to cheer them up, then – that's just the kind of guy I am."

~*~

Frances lowers her aeros onto my hotel's rooftop parking lot. Baltimore zips all around us, brimming with activity. It's late afternoon, but I'm completely exhausted from today's sojourn into Steam. My aluminum cane is between my legs, a constant reminder of how weak I am in the real world, a reminder of what I really am and the choice I made. Forced nerve regrowth and stem cell therapy has come a long way. Still, cybernetic replacements would have left me cane-free. A man has to stick to his convictions, even if they kill him.

I raise my hand to fix my hair and remember that I only have a little peach fuzz on my dome. It'd be nice to be able to change my hairstyle on a whim, as I'm able to do in a Proxima World. The more I exist in the real world, the more I wish to be as far away from it as possible. Maybe this is the plight of humanity playing out in my tiny, insignificant life. Maybe we are destined towards distraction, which VE dreamworlds ultimately supply. What is the end of our distraction? When do we simply become brains in a vat thinking our existences alive?

Strong thoughts from a worldly weakling.

"You've been quiet," I say, turning to Frances. Someone needs to say something and I figure that someone is me.

"I just need some rest," she says, yawning.

"You sure you're okay?"

"I'm fine."

"You want to come up?" I nod to the hotel.

Frances Euphoria cuts me down with a cold stare. "Why?"

"We could watch some *Maltese Falcon*; we never finished it."

"I think I need to head home," she says. "I'll pick you up in the morning."

I'm out of her little HondaFord aeros seconds later, watching her lift into the sky. She waits for the appropriate airlane to become available and sails away, disappearing into the swarm of vehicles above Baltimore.

Taking it slowly, I walk into the hotel through the sliding glass doors. The lobby is expansive, complete with tiny indoor pavilions separated by frosted motoglass. They're pod-like, meant to facilitate business meetings, illicit and otherwise, as well as a place for the wealthy travelers to rest their heads while the room is prepared, or while their flight is delayed. If I were in The Loop I would set this place ablaze just for the hell of it – that's my mood as I make my way to the elevator.

I'm just about to press the elevator's button when I remember something. A Humandroid hotel hospitality team member walks by and I stop him.

"I'd like to place an order for room service," I say.

"I'm sorry, sir, order taking isn't one of my functions."

"So you're completely unable to take an order? That's entirely beyond the scope of your abilities? There's absolutely no way you can take an order? Too good to extend hospitality to hotel guests, are you?"

"If I may, sir – you can place an order over iNet on the elevator ride to your room. It's quite simple."

I look the droid over – black vest, white shirt with a black bowtie, damn near translucent skin, hair like a movie star. His eyes give him away. They are truly soulless, mirrors into a brain made of wiring, not tissue.

"Over iNet?"

"Yes, sir, over iNet."

"I don't like using iNet. How about placing an order for me? I need, no want, no need is fine – I need two beers and some type of appetizer delivered to my room. The name is Quantum Hughes. Got it?"

"Yes … sir … " If he is annoyed by me he's not showing it. "What type of appetizer would you like?"

"Do you have quesadillas?"

"We do."

"Well, sign me up for two."

"Two slices of quesadilla?"

No, two *full* quesadillas."

He scans me up and down, just like Robocop Mark9 did. "Sir, based on your height, mass, metabolic rate and body type, the caloric content of two full quesadillas represents one hundred thirty percent of your recommended daily intake."

"My what?"

A hot broad passes by and I shoot her a wink. She ignores me and continues.

"The FDA recently passed new federal guidelines for the enjoyment of Mexican food."

"Are you pulling my leg?"

The Humandroid looks shocked. "No, sir, I am simply informing you of the FDA's recent federal guidelines. Due to the high fat and sodium content of Mexican food as consumed by Americans, guidelines have been put into place to help reduce the deleterious consequences of over-consumption."

"So I can't have two quesadillas?"

"You can, but it is highly inadvisable and I'll have to flag your account to the FDA Monitoring Group, who will likely send you an iNet message reminding you to eat healthy."

"You're shitting me."

"Unlikely sir. I do not excrete my waste products as do human beings, and I'm afraid that you represent far too large a bolus for me to pass." His expression remains carefully neutral.

I raise my eyebrow at the droid, and just for a moment I channel the spirit of Moe Howard. "A wise guy, eh?"

"Not at all, sir, I am performing my assigned duty in the friendliest and most informative, assistive manner possible."

"Well excellent then. If it's not too much bother, do you think that you could get me two quesadillas extra cheese, two large beers, a side order of bacon, and a shaker of bad cholesterol? And bill the people paying for my room, the FCG. No man, machine or federal entity will tell me how many quesadillas I can enjoy. Over my dead body."

"There is a zero-carb, organic, no saturated fat option … "

~*~

*~I hope they don't hang you, precious, by that sweet neck. Yes, angel, I'm gonna send you over. The chances are you'll get off with life. That means if you're a good girl, you'll be out in twenty years. I'll be waiting for you. If they hang you, I'll always remember you.*

I'm on my bed watching *The Maltese Falcon* when I hear a knock at the door. I open it, and barely make eye contact with a different friendly, informative, assistive Humandroid hospitality team member who's holding a stainless steel serving tray with two frosty-cold forty ounce bottles of barley pop in an ice bucket and an insulated dome covered dish. Dinner is served.

"Are both of these for you, sir?" he asks.

133

"What, are you the big quesadilla sheriff of the house? The head *Über Sturm Quesadilla Führer* of the FDA's calorie Nazis? Yes – they're *both* for me."

"Sir, FDA guidelines … "

"Shut up."

"Sir, I need a verbal confirmation that you realize the risks of eating Mexican food in this quantity."

"Risks?" I almost laugh. "All right, droid here's your verbal confirmation – *I'm aware of the risks*. Now give me my food."

"Sir, the chef regrets to inform you that a shaker of bad cholesterol is unavailable, so he included an extra side order of bacon." He hands me the tray.

"Tell him I said thanks."

I take the tray from him and let the door slam shut behind me. Sticky, gooey cheesy quesadillas find their way into my mouth. I munch the grilled chicken bits, cilantro, onions and bell peppers, and enjoy the flavors as they carpet bomb my taste buds. The bacon is a nice crispy addition, and it all goes especially well with the cheap beer. I reflect that Chef at the Mondegreen probably has *two* shakers of bad cholesterol in his kitchen. *The bastard.*

One brewski later and I'm feeling good, heavy, but good – the slight buzz is comforting, nerve-calming. With the flick on the tube and my belly full of Mexican food, I'm a happy camper, a man at rest. I'm about to take the first sip of my second beer when my eyes dart from the screen to the NV Visor.

A large gulp later and I'm standing, slowly making my way over to the haptic chair. I relax onto the chair, staring across the room at my bed, at the silver tray, topped with a few plastic salsa containers and the gnawed corpse of the second quesadilla. Another sip from my beer. The bottle is indeed half-full or half-empty, depending on how you look at it. Me? I'm a half-empty guy, so I go ahead and down the rest.

I relax onto the haptic chair, place the NV Visor over my face, and listen for the Brian Eno tone. Sine waves appear on the inside of the visor and dance like octopi during a tsunami. I'm familiar with what happens next. If I keep the visor on, I'll eventually drift off and I'll be able to select a Proxima World from my preferred list. I can dive to any world, but some worlds are exclusive, some have a membership cost and some, like The Loop, are archival worlds – dead worlds. They still exist, but they're no longer advertised or known by the masses. This was why I never saw a human player in The Loop until I met Frances – people can't readily find archival worlds, as there are hundreds and they are buried in the stack. Further, worlds with glitches are immediately closed by the Proxima Network, which means it takes some hacking to get into them.

Luckily, The Loop is one of my preferred worlds.

"Here goes nothing," I say as I relax further into the haptic chair.

# Chapter Ten

Feedback a blessing, a reminder. Feedback the sound I heard for months upon months; a curio, an artifact of existence, a denotation of being, a curse. A breath of digital air while staring up at a darkened cloud brings a cheek-shattering smile to my face. I've spawned somewhere near Three King's Park, the mangled trees accented by lightning, shiny from the constant downpour. Riotous fiends hover around a trashcan fire, shivering, warming their paws. Peddling bootblacks or mucky vagabonds by day, perma-fried parasites with arms covered in spider bites and pants filled with ticks – psychonauts are the roaches of The Loop, if you find one, you'd damn well better know there's another.

*Home Sweet Home.*

I have the notion to whip out my BFG 9000, item 100, and plasmatize the bastards, but I suppress it. There will be plenty of time to maim at a later date.

My hand comes up and a taxi lowers.

Before the NPC driver can say anything, I access my S&W .500, item 466.

"What's the big idea, Mac?" the driver – fat, surly, unshaven, cigar-chomping – asks, as he looks down the barrel of my über-shooter.

"You're out, I'm in," I say motioning to the door. "Scram."

"Fat chance. I'm not gettin' out in this neighborhood, Mac."

"Suit yourself."

I pull the trigger, shattering the driver's side window. His head splashes, makes a mess *largo*. "Sorry, bub," I say as I lug his corpse out of the vehicle. "I gave you fair warning."

As soon as he's out, I equip my hotel towel, item 13, and wipe the blood off the inside of the front windshield. A crimsoned window never stopped me before – but being in the real world for a month has civilized me. Imagine that.

Hands on the yoke and I lift off, aiming the vehicle towards The Mondegreen Hotel. The sky opens up and I flick the windshield wipers on. Cold rain whips into the taxi through the shattered driver's side window, soaking my clothes. I catch my own eyes in the rearview mirror and my blond hair fixes itself. A black suit appears on my body and my tie loosens. I've got a date with destiny and I want to look good.

I'm at the Mondegreen a few minutes later, lowering the aeros into the shit-stained street outside the hotel. Excitement ripples through me; razor-winged butterflies nearly break free from my stomach. It's like I just had my first kiss or something. I hop up the stairs leading to the hotel and swing the doors open.

"Mr. Hughes?" Doorman Jim runs his hand along the front of his jacket, clears his throat. "I … we, weren't expecting you. Did you make a reservation?"

"Yeah, I made a reservation," I say, accessing my inventory list behind my back. A quick scroll and item 501, my Beretta 92 with a silencer appears in my hand.

"Mr. Hughes, please!"

"Just kidding, old pal," I say, lowering the gun. "Also, it's Quantum."

"Right! Mr. Quantum, will you be … dining here tonight?"

I raise the gun again and give him a third eye for old times' sake. Might as well toast the milquetoast.

~*~

First things first. I enter the dining room and move straight to the kitchen.

"Hello you old bastard!" I say as I kick open the door, meat cleaver in one hand and a turkey baster filled with Chernobyl reactor melt in the other (items 123 and 348, respectively). The plump chef is in front of the stove, whistling *Always Look on the Bright Side of Life.*

"Quantum!" he says with a grin. "You've come for pancakes?"

"Not exactly ... "

"THEN YOU'VE COME TO DIE!"

Chef throws a ladle full of piping hot soup. I *bullet time* backwards out of its trajectory, activate advanced abilities and execute a *grand jeté* just as he tips the five gallons of Cream of Hot Death Soup over the spot I've just vacated. I land like a springbok, step into a side kick and go right on my ass as I slide in the soup.

"Ha!" he shouts, "I have you now!" He pulls big heavy pots and pans from the overhead rack and pelts me with them. I regain my feet just as he throws a handful of Thai curry powder in my face. He hammers me with right-cross, left-hook, elbow, elbow and a mean head-butt. Apparently, he's been practicing.

"Is that all you got?" he mocks, "I thought you'd have way more game than this. I fart in your general direction!" Chef comes for me wielding a meat mallet the size of a post maul, and as he brings it up and around to cube my steak, I lunge and jam the turkey baster up his nose and into his brain, squeeze the bulb and fill his skull with fissile Ukrainian yumminess. He drops like a rock, flames shoot out of his ears and his eyes glow green, bubble, and melt.

"I'm not cleaning that up!" says the Saucier, a pencil-neck geek of a guy whom I usually ignore.

I return to the dining area feeling like a badass. That's one thing I *don't* feel like in the real world – with my cane and my slight limp, just about anyone can take me on, from a toddler in a stroller to an emphysematic grandmother in a Hoveround. In the Proxima Galaxy I feel strong, amplified, invincible, like my old self. Nothing beats it.

I plop down in the same spot I sat for years on end. I'm in the far corner of the dining room, with a wall behind me, allowing me to watch the entrance and the kitchen as well as the windows. One can never check six too often The Loop.

A light appears in front of me and Dolly materializes. She's in a red dress, her hair in a bob, her lips the color of blood, her nails red, the diamond necklace I gave her around her neck. My heart melts as soon as I lay eyes on her.

"You … came back," she says softly.

"You knew I was here the moment I logged in," I remind her, just to say something.

She smiles. "I wanted to see where you'd go first, here or Barfly's."

I laugh just to cover the tears of joy I feel coming on, something I've rarely felt in a Proxima World. Everything in the dining room has a sharp gleam to it now, as if I'm in the den of an angel. "You know me too well, too well, Doll."

"So what do ya want?" She asks, an order pad appearing in her hand. "The usual?"

"I've missed you," I say, the words fumbling out of my mouth. "I can't describe how much I missed you, but, but … I've missed everything about you, Dolly. Your being, your face, your eyes. Everything."

"Really?" She drops the pad.

"Everything, seriously."

The surroundings pixilate and we're in my old hotel room, the same room I woke up in for two subjective years straight. On the wall is the picture of the sinking sailboat. My sheets are ruffled as they always were; a pack of cigarettes sits on the nightstand.

Dolly falls into my arms. Her weight, her aura – all are realer than anything I've experienced in the last month. We kiss and I feel my skin ripple with goose bumps. Another kiss and I can't even think about undressing. Lost in the moment and feeling her lips against mine and her body pressed into my chest and her hands around the back of my neck pulling me in closer, closer.

"I missed you so much," she says through her kisses. "More than … more than anything."

"I'm sorry," I say, thinking of what happened between Frances and me, thinking of how I've been avoiding The Loop. "I'm so sorry, Dolly. I can't … I can't exist without you. I'm sorry for making you wait."

"You *are* my world," she says, her eyes filling with sorrow. "I don't care where you're from or how different we truly are. In here, you're my world, and we consist … " She kisses me almost harshly, biting at my lip. "In here we are the same, we are the lightning, we are … " More kisses. "We are one."

~*~

I reach for my deck of Luckies on the nightstand; stick a smoky treat in my face and suck in as it ignites. My lungs fill and my simulated algorithmic nicotine receptors scream with pleasure like schoolgirls on rollercoaster. The smoke swirls and eddies against the ceiling when I blow out. Dolly is next to me, her naked body pressed into mine. She reaches up, plucks the cigarette from my lips, drags on it, coughs.

I laugh and she pulls the blanket to her chest. "What?" she asks, and smiles. "I always cough when I smoke with you."

"I remember," I tell her, "That's what I'm laughing about, the memories we share and … " I try to verbalize how I'm feeling at the moment but it's impossible. There are simply too many emotions colliding around the room, zipping through my skull and zigzagging through my nervous system for me to say how I truly feel.

She lets the blanket drop and I pull her in closer. Holding her tight, I take another drag from the cigarette. My problems in other worlds – the real world, Steam – come to me in a series of flashes. I exhale my problems, letting them dissipate with the cloud of blue smoke in front of me.

"What are you thinking about?" she asks.

141

"Don't worry about it."

Her hand comes to my face. "You want to watch a movie or something?"

"No, I need to get out," I say. "Get active."

"We could go to Barfly's … " she suggests.

"We've never gone together before … "

"That settles it then." She stands and takes a few steps to the center of the room. Her skin is porcelain, her naked body a Renaissance sculpture. "What should I wear?" she asks, looking at me over her shoulder.

"How about nothing?" I suggest as I take in her curves.

"Quantum … "

"What? Who's gonna stop you? You're the NVA Seed – you rule here. You are The Loop's Cleopatra." I blow her a kiss. "Wear whatever you'd like, Doll."

"No, I want wear whatever *you'd* like."

"I like you best how you are right now."

"What are you going to wear?"

"All black."

"Black it is then."

A strapless black dress appears on her body. In her hand is a tiny Flapper purse and on her feet are strappy black high heels with red soles. "This okay?"

I wolf whistle. "It's more than just okay, Doll," and she smiles like we're off to the Junior Prom.

~*~

No need to hail a taxi when your main squeeze is the NVA Seed.

With the snap of her fingers, we're in front of the entrance to Barfly's, the dive of dives usually filled with ossified lounge lizards, blasted boozehounds, card sharks and everything in between. Murky characters dip in and out of the shadows – addicts high off Riotous drooling down their fronts as they thumb their noses at passing working girls in skin-tight dresses and pleather jackets. I look up at the neon floozie in the Martini glass, her legs scissoring, electric bubbles popping over her head. One, two, three. Repeat sequence.

Croc the doorman takes one hard look at me and shakes his head.

"You got something to say?" I ask the big man with fists as large as cinder blocks.

His scowl turns into a grin. "Where ya been, Quantum? You found a better joint or something?"

"There are no better joints, Croc. Been busy."

"Too busy to come to Barfly's?"

"Did I forget to pay my tab or something? Why are you giving me the third degree?"

Croc's eyes skip from Dolly's face to mine. "I never knew … "

143

Dolly says, "Quantum has been away, but he's back now."

"I get it," the big man says, sizing me up. His muscles are practically bursting out of his shirt, his deeply pockmarked cheeks cast shadows that point towards his chin. "It's nice to go away, but it's always nice to return home."

"They say home is where the heart is." I nod to Dolly. "Maybe they're right."

The big man lets us pass without patting me down. The inventory list restriction that was once in place is no longer active, so it wouldn't matter if he patted me down anyway. As soon as we enter, I spot Cid behind the bar, grizzled and chiseled in a battered fedora, wiping something up with a yellow rag. The rest of the gin mill is pretty much the same, from the jukebox in the corner to the pool tables, one of which is covered in beer stains.

"I invited some of your friends," Dolly says as soon as we sit down at the bar.

"My friends?"

A familiar uproar behind me sends a half-smile across my face.

"Oi, Mates! There's the la-di-da poofter now!" a man shouts from across the room in a crap Dick Van Dyke accent. "And look at the smashing bit o' stuff 'e just walked in with!"

"Ya bloody great clodpoll! That's not *a bit o' stuff*, that's '*Erself*!"

"Oh, Clucking Bell, so it is! Ever so sorry, Ma'am!"

Dolly smiles, waves, blows them a kiss.

"Bloody hell! Let him buy the next round! Am I *wrang*?"

"A meringue?"

"What's a meringue got to do with anything!?"

"What's that? Have a go?"

"Shut yer geggy!"

I turn to find the six UK Assassins playing snooker amidst a solid pile of empty mugs and sideways shot glasses. Irish Shorty, Burly, Pip, Scotty, Bucket Hat and the Quiet Man are clad in their Iraq War garb, from Scotty's tan-brown-black kilt to Pip's face paint.

"Next round is on me!" says Bucket Hat.

"Oi! Watch your bloody elbow, mate! You almost spilt beer on me trousers!"

"Well, keep yer bloody trews away from me beer!"

Part of me wants to laugh, the other part of me wants to select General Thompson's eponymous shootin' iron – item 247 – and declare my independence.

"What'll it be, Quantum?" Cid asks with a bottle of Jack Daniel's Silver Select in one hand and a pair of frosty-cold Löwenbräu Oktoberfestbiers in the other. He's a big ol' boy, but he's all forearm – more Popeye than Bluto.

"Glenfiddich all around!" Burly says, next to me now with his finger in the air. "We thought you'd never come back, Quantum."

"Well, here I am."

Pip and Scotty are on the pool table now, rolling over one another as they scramble to land the first slug. *Snap!* The Quiet Man reverses his cue stick, tests it for balance, and breaks it across Pip's back.

"What was *that*? My poor, aged Nursie strikes with more authority than that!"

"Jorum of skee 'ere's to glee!" Burly foregoes pouring the shot into a shot glass and slaps the bottle in my hand. I tip it in a salute, raise it to my lips, and take to it like a baby to McStarbuck's Genuine Synthetic Kosher-Vegan-Halal Almond-Soy Breast Milk Substitute. "That's me boy, that is!" Burley says, clapping me on the back.

"Nothing like getting zozzled with the old, honored enemy!" I say as I put my arm around Dolly's waist.

Pip and Scotty have stopped fighting now and are arm over shoulder singing, *"One pleasant evening in the month of June, As I was sitting with my glass and spoon, A small bird sat on an ivy bunch, And the song he sang was The Jug of Punch!"*

Burly rips the bottle from my hand and takes a monster swig. "That'll do," he says with a sigh, "that'll do."

"Where's Aiden?" I ask Dolly, already feeling the effects of the giggle water.

"Here."

Morning Assassin appears behind the bar, in a black apron and a white collared shirt. My hand comes up and he grabs it. I pull him in close, our elbows on the bar now as if we're arm wrestling.

"What the hell are you doing back there?" I ask with a growl.

"Waiting to kill you."

"Well, go ahead and do it already, Bucko."

He raises a bottle with his other hand.

146

"That's the best you can do? I've got a forty watt phased plasma rifle with your name written all over it."

His hand tightens around mine. "Oh yeah? Well I have a chainsaw under the bar."

"A chainsaw I gave you!" I say, laughing. Burly wraps his arm around my shoulder and shoves the whiskey bottle back in my hand. I tilt my head back, throw more of Barfly's surprisingly high quality gargle down my neck and keep an eye on Aiden. One can never be too safe in The Loop.

I finish the bottle and burp. "Damn, it's nice to see you," I say, letting go of Morning Assassin's hand.

"Same Quantum," he says. "So are we getting thoroughly ethylated tonight or what?"

"That's the plan!"

"Two bottles of whiskey," he tells Cid the bartender, "the best you got."

"You paying?" I ask. "I'm not made of mazuma."

"I'll put it on your tab," says Cid, tipping his fedora at me.

## Chapter Eleven

Light cuts through the drapes. Feedback fills the space between here and there, glitterbombing the inside of my cranium. I blink my peepers open and the feedback sprays from my ears, champagne showering the mattress and nearly popping my head off the pillow. Feedback an old friend that deserves a kick in the jewels; feedback a salesman with one hand in your pocket and the other around your neck.

"Where ... ?"

One look at the water-stained ceiling tells me exactly where I am. My hotel room at the Mondegreen. Instinct takes over and I wince-roll out of bed. Morning Assassin will be here any minute and I'd better be ready for him. Inventory list. My AR 15 appears in my hands, item 58. I pop the magazine in and pull back the charging handle, feeding a round into the chamber.

Through blurred vision, I sit with my back against the bed and my assault rifle aimed at the window. The window smashes and glass peppers the air. Like clockwork, Morning Assassin rolls in carrying a plastic bag full of cactuses and a bottle of lemon juice.

"A bag of cactuses?" I ask skeptically.

"Don't forget the lemon juice." He squirts the bottle. "I figured it'd hurt more."

We both start laughing.

"That's not a bad weapon."

"I get bored in here without my arch nemesis."

"I know the feeling."

"How's the real world, anyway?" he asks as he sits down on the corner of my bed.

"That's a damn good question. I should be there right now; I'm sure Frances Euphoria is on her way to my hotel to pick me up."

"How is she?"

"Mean as ever. She ain't a redhead in the real world though; she has short brown hair."

Aiden says, "I can't imagine her like that."

"You're telling me. Stranger than fiction up there."

"So that's why you're here?"

I'm silent for a moment as I process his question. "I guess it *is* why I'm here," I finally say. "I was two beers in last night after a day in a different Proxima World and I figured what the hell. Plus, there is a pair of Feds giving me a hard time up there. I guess I just wanted to escape, needed to escape."

"Sometimes it's all we can do." Aiden's brown eyes flicker as he says this.

"How do you escape in here?"

"Three Kings Park, watch some flicks, head off to The Pier to check on Dirty Dave. Get a massage in Chinatown. You know, the usual."

"He still making weapons out there?" I ask.

"He is. Why? You need something custom?"

"Maybe. I'm having issues in this Proxima World called Steam. They penalize my life bar if I have anything that isn't world appropriate. You should see how obsessive these steampunkers are about keeping to their rules."

"Steampunkers?"

"Long story. Think no electricity in a futuristic Victorian setting. They can have weapons as long as they aren't electric, which rules out some of my better toys. Well, I suppose they can be electric, but it must be powered by steam. Also, my mutant hacks, the ones you traded me for that chainsaw, don't seem to have any effects on the Steam Enforcers."

"Steam Enforcers?"

"Big robots five stories tall with enough armor to give an armadillo a stiffy."

"So you need something world appropriate to take these enforcers down?"

"Bingo."

"Dirty Dave's Mayhem Mart?" he suggests.

"What are we waiting for?

"Repopulating hack it is." Aiden extends his arm to me and I latch on.

~*~

Everything pixilates into view. The sun is still in the sky above The Pier, adding a sheen to the oily waters. The water lashes at the sides of the dock and spills over, signaling that a storm is brewing. A storm is always brewing in The Loop, the vice-ridden netherworld's belly of the beast.

"Quantum."

Dolly steps out of a sudden burst of light, still in her black dress. This quickly morphs into something more Pier appropriate – a pair of tight black jeans, a black V-neck t-shirt and black slippers.

"Where did you go last night?" I ask. I still haven't pieced together how I got back to the hotel, but I assume Dolly had a part in it.

"You were drinking with your friends; I decided to let you have your fun."

"So how did I get back to the hotel?"

Aiden raises his eyebrows. "That would be my doing."

"Wait a damn minute … how many days have I been in The Loop?" I have the notion to pull up my inventory list and find my logout point, item 555, the star-shaped piece of paper that allowed me to finally leave the City of Filth.

"Relax. Everything is fine in the real world. It's morning there," Dolly says, "same time as it is here. Logging back in yesterday reset everything. The glitch no longer exists. If it did, you still have the logout point."

"Frances will be at my hotel soon."

Her eyes dart away. "Forget reality. I'm here to help you with your weapons issue, so you can get a leg up in this *other* Proxima World."

"How did you … " I turn to Aiden. "Just how much information do you two share with each other?"

"She sees everything I see, hears everything I hear." A smile twitches across his face.

"Is this … the same for you, Dolly?"

"No," she says, reading the look of apprehension on my face. "Our lovemaking sessions are private.

Aiden cracks up.

"Keep it up, pal," I tell him. "You might find your foot in a bear trap and a Molotov cocktail up your ass."

His hands come up. "Take it easy, buddy. If I could come to your world, I'd be chasing tail as well."

"Chasing tail?" Dolly asks.

Something moves in the corner of my eye. Two bleached people in collars appear, snarling and barking at us. A man and a woman – both with skin melted off their skeletal frames, both with zombiesque patches of hair covering their skulls. Just for show, I equip my newest weapon, the Slice Bang, part blade and part shotty.

More bleached people surge over a stack of shipping crates. They bite at each other, seethe and claw. They are hungry corpses, rabid animals in grotesque human form.

"They're still here?" I ask, twisting my Slice Bang in front of me. I can tell by the look on Aiden's face that he'd like to take her for a test drive.

"I was meaning to talk to you about that … " Dolly frowns, points at them and the bleached people freeze. "The Reapers left them here."

"Left them? How many?"

Their forms waver, as if they're seconds away from shattering their bonds.

"Ninety-five."

"All in The Pier?"

"Some have spread to other places."

"Can't you two kill them?"

Aiden says, "We *can* kill them, but they just respawn. Trust me; I've spent the better part of a week hunting them."

"But I thought they died in the real world if they were killed in a Proxima World … "

"Yes," Dolly says, as tiny sparks of electricity ripple through their forms, "but only if *you* kill them, a human player."

I offer my Slice Bang to Aiden, grip first, blade across my forearm – I saw J.E.B. Stuart do it in a 2-D docudrama and I thought it looked cool. "Have at it, amigo. I have enough problems in the real world."

"You serious?" he asks, testing the weight and balance of the Slice Bang.

"*Yahoo Serious*? Oh NO! Did they get him too?"

153

"Nice one," he snorts. "May I?"

"By all means, get you some."

His face sprouts a predatory grin. "Unfreeze them."

For the next minute or so, I watch him slice and bang his way through the small crowd of lost souls. He pivots right, his blade spilling the guts of a bleached person while another tries to latch onto his neck. Shotgun to the face and that one is now digitally extinct. Grandstanding, M.A. flips backwards into the air, landing on a man's shoulders. Aiden is at his best in the midst of sheer butchery; the look of unalloyed pleasure on his face convinces me that some people – people like me, people like him – never change.

The only old dog learning new tricks here is the one lying on the ground in a puddle of his own blood.

~\*~

Aiden takes care of biz and returns.

"Geez Aiden," I say. "Shove a shiv in Shiva and call you the Doombringer. You remind me of … *me!*"

"I'll take that as a compliment." He grins, obviously pleased. He twists his wrist and examines the Slice-Bang from several angles. "Nice piece of kit, by the way." In a slick application of digital prestidigitation, he produces an orange shop rag and cleans the blood from the blade, which I think is a polite gesture and the hallmark of a true

154

craftsman caring for the tools of his trade. "Not too heavy, the right sized blade and the shotty – what other types of weapons do they have in Steam?"

"Lots of stuff like this," I say as we enter one of the warehouses.

Chains hang above us, suspended from loops and pulleys attached to the ceiling. An ancient conveyer belt collects dust behind a stack of boxes green with mold. There are shitholes and then there are the warehouses in The Pier.

"You know you can bring us with you to Steam," Dolly says. "I gave you the seed. Did you forget about that already?"

Aiden doesn't say anything, but I can tell by the way that he's looking at me that he'd love a change of pace. *Who wouldn't?*

"I'll have to think about that."

M.A's hands come to the sides of his face and he shouts, "Dave, open up! I'm here with some friends."

"Last time I stopped by he had guards and ED-209s."

Aiden shrugs. "I guess he downgraded, by choice or by force."

"Yup, I've been there before," I say, thinking of the time I spent hooked on Riotous. It's a good thing they don't have that shit in the real world.

Dolly's squeezes my hand. "Can't you just make Dirty Dave appear?" I ask her.

"I can, but I try to avoid doing that. I like giving NPCs as much freedom as possible. It keeps things interesting."

"Well, I have some plans in the real world, that's why I'm asking."

155

"With Frances?"

"Yeah, but not like that. It's strictly work. We've got to dive back into Steam, and they kicked our asses and took our lunch money last time. I need better weapons."

Her lips press together. She's mollified some, but not all the way.

"I wouldn't ask if it wasn't important."

She gives me a long, hard look, and sighs a deep sigh that moves her mammiferous attributes in a most distracting way. "All right," she says. "Because it's work, and because it's important, and because it's you that asks."

She twitches her nose, and Dirty Dave steps out of the shadows. There's something rat-like about him. Maybe it's his buckteeth and his beady little eyes, his scraggly beard or the way he holds his hands in front of his body as if he were latching on to a giant bread crumb. His mouth opens but no words come out. His body odor is stupefying; it would knock a buzzard off a shit wagon at fifty yards; even the flies won't come near him.

"Geez Louise, Davey Boy, ol' friend, ol'pal, ol' stick-in-the-mud," I say. "I've seen you look a whole lot better. How much of that Riotous are you doing?"

"Riotous?" He bares his teeth to me – sharp, yellow, brittle. They look like someone has knit tiny individual brownish-green sweaters for each of them. "You have? *You give.*" His shoulders come up; his dilated eyes fixate on me.

"C'mon Dave! It's your old pal, Quantum! Is this how you welcome an old friend?"

Dolly steps forward and the NPC's mouth snaps shut. One look from her and Dirty Dave is minding his Ps and Qs.

Aiden steps up to the plate. "Dave, we need a weapon that can cut through ensorcelled metal."

I pipe in. "Dave, I got big giant magic metal robots five stories tall that nothing I got will touch. You know what I have; all the wowsie-wow stuff came from you." He smiles and grunts at that; at least some of the weaponsmaster is still in there somewhere. "They're in a different Proxima world, different rules – so, no electricity although steam-powered analog is okay. No lasers, no high tech; I need something organic, maybe. Something natural, something low-tech and non-electric that'll cut through magicked metal."

"Metal ... Magic ... " Dave bites at his nails, blinks rapidly. He mutters to himself, scratches ass, armpits, crotch; belches, sharts in his already befouled trousers. "Yes, I have something. AUS."

I sigh. This is a great big fat waste of time. "A US? A US what?"

"No. Ay You Ess. Almost Universal Solvent. Dissolves everything 'cept gold. Cheap and easy to make. Not cheap and easy to store once made, but completely inert until last two ingredients mixed."

"Oh – kaay, how do I use it?"

"Easy to weaponize. Back pack sprayer, two tanks, one with each of last two ingredients. Ingredients mix in gold nozzle, propelled by $CO_2$ or steam."

"Good. What will it cost?"

Dirty Dave's hand comes behind his back. He glances from me to Dolly.

"How much Riotous?" I ask.

"Fifty."

"Fifty?"

"Fifty pounds. Pure. Uncut."

"You're really looking to set the record straight, aren't ya?" I turn to Dolly. "Can you make this happen?"

"Normally I don't … "

"Forty pounds and I won't kill you, take your stuff, and go push the Riotous in Three Kings Park." I tell Dave.

He nods excitedly.

"Dolly?" Taking her hand in mine, I give her that *just this once* look.

"Fine, Quantum," she says, her brow furrowing. "But let's not make a habit of it."

I turn back to the bug-eyed hop-head. "How long will this take?"

"Two hours, tops."

"Swell. Aiden can deliver it to me."

"Deliver it?" he asks.

"That's right, you can deliver it to me there, in Steam."

A grin spreads across his face. "In that case, I'll get your Slice Bang modified as well."

"Modded?"

"What about AUS shotgun shells?" Aiden asks Dirty Dave. "Yes or no?"

The scabrous little tweaker gives him the thumbs up.

"And Dolly … "

"Yes?" she asks.

"I want you to get some weapons made as well."

"How many?"

"Six sets, just in case we need a little back-up."

~*~

A sudden flash and Dolly and I are back in my hotel room. The bed is made, the window that Aiden smashed earlier has been repaired.

"Reading my mind?" I ask as I pull her into my arms.

"Will you come back?" she asks instead of kissing me. "To The Loop, to me – will you?"

"I'm bringing you with me, babe, to Steam."

"I know, but this … this is our place, this room, this world. It's ours." Tears form in the corners of her eyes. "It's for you … I exist for you."

159

"There is only one world that isn't our place," I say before realizing how harsh my statement sounds. "That's not what I mean, what I mean is that there are … thousands of worlds for us to explore."

"I can only exist in your dreams."

"What separates a dream from reality, Doll? Who's to say I'm not dreaming when I'm awake up there? Who's to say that it isn't a sham, an elaborate hoax? I existed in a dream with you for eight years, *eight years.* For those eight years our dream, my dream, was real, was one – just like you said. And this trip … this has really forced me to think about the world up there. It's as much of a dream as a Proxima World, governed by laws, physical and legal."

"But you're *alive* up there, alive."

"I am, and you're alive here."

She pushes away from me.

"But I'm also alive here; I feel more alive in a Proxima World than I do the real world – coming here has reminded me of this. We can, we should, just enjoy each other in these worlds. We can travel anywhere, do anything."

She puts her arms around my neck, her face against my chest. Her tears make a damp spot on my shirt.

"I am a man of several worlds, but my heart is yours, Doll. Coming back has reminded me of this, reminded me of what it feels like to be truly happy."

# Chapter Twelve

Logging out.

Still it amazes me that I can log out of The Loop, that I can move freely between the two worlds.

My hands come to my NV Visor. There's a ring of sweat on my forehead and my back is stiff. I've been out for at least ten hours, no fourteen, and while I feel refreshed due to the fact I was essentially sleeping, I'm also on edge. Sitting up with a cringe, I manually move my legs to the floor so blood can fill them.

The numbness is prickly, funny in its own way. I flick my calf just to feel the half-dead limb. It takes another minute before I'll trust my legs to support my weight. I know I shouldn't, I've been avoiding mirrors for some time; as soon as I can move with a reasonable assurance of not face planting, I move to the restroom to take in my reflection and, of course, drain the lizard.

My reflection.

My hair is starting to grow back and I've gained a little weight. Dark circles under my eyes add depth to my skull; my nose is more defined in the real world than it is in the The Loop. I remove my shirt and notice that I still have a few lingering bruises in various shades of purple and yellow; nearly the same hues as the color scheme of my room at the Mondegreen. Maybe I'm not getting enough vitamins. Maybe I'm just getting old.

I lean in closer to my reflection and observe the subtle blemishes on my cheeks, the blackheads on the sides of my nose. *This* is detail, detail that I've never noticed in a VE dreamworld. If the Proxima Company could replicate this level of detail …

I blink and a message splashes across my eyelids.

Frances: Outside. Are you coming?

I think the words and strangely enough, they appear.

Me: No, just breathing hard. Maintain a firm grasp on the equines; I'll be right there.

France: The what?

Me: Hold your horses.

There's another message: *Guide to a Healthier You: Avoiding Hazards Associated with Exceeding the Adult Daily Recommended Caloric Intake,* from the Fat Nazis – as opposed to the fat Nazis – I suppose. Why would they think that anyone would read this? I mark the sender as *toxic spammer* and delete the message unread.

I put my shirt back on and I'm nearly out the door when I notice a subtle hint of *Eau de Cab Driver's Revenge* emanating from somewhere. One sniff at my armpit quickly identifies the culprit. Quick about face into the bathroom. I give face, armpits, and naughty bits a quick once-over with a damp facecloth, vigorously swish a mouthful of ListerCope *Cool Arctic Spearmint Tsunami* to knock the fur off my teeth, and liberally spray myself down with Wrightguard *Baja Mountain Estrus* body spray in the special *Wilbur & Orville Commemorative Package.*

162

Now, if the advertisements are to be believed, I'll be forced to fend off hordes of unusually attractive, large-breasted nubile women of child-bearing age who want nothing more than to procreate with me, repeatedly.

I exit to the landing stage, and the horde consists of a disgruntled Frances, who gives me a very credible stink-eye and pointedly taps her wristwatch-free wrist as I walk up to her aeros.

~*~

She sniffs two or three times and makes the *Who's Got a Poopy Shoe* face as I settle into the passenger's seat and harness up.

"I dove last night," I tell Frances Euphoria to forestall that whole line of observational commentary that she's no doubt about to entertain me with.

"To Cyber Noir?"

"Yes, to *The Loop.*"

"Good for you!" she says as her aeros lifts into the proper airlane. The morning sun sends an arc of bright light through the windshield.

"What did you do in there?" she asks.

"Went to Barfly's, saw some old friends, met a weapons manufacturer." I tell her, purposely leaving out Dolly.

"A weapons manufacturer?"

"Dirty Dave's Mayhem Mart, down by The Pier. The dirtiest gun hawker you'll find in The Loop as long as he isn't hopped up on Riotous. If he can't make it, he can procure it. I figured I could use some custom-made gear in Steam."

"Did you buy me anything?"

I tense up, knowing I just broke the Hamburger Rule: Don't get your meat at the same place you get your bread. "About that … "

"I'm sure all your assassin buddies got something."

"What makes you so sure?" I ask.

"Well, did they?"

"They did … " My stomach grumbles. "But only because Aiden was there, calling the shots. I'll say this – it was Aiden's fault. From there, I plead the Fifth."

"Is that so? Aiden's fault?"

My eyes move from the front of our vehicle to the side window. I recall the Reapers ramming their aeros into ours a few days back. What would have happened if they'd taken our vehicle down? Neither Frances nor I have really spoken about the incident. Clearly we needed to tell someone, but how could we prove it? This thought gives me a chance to deflect the animosity currently aimed in my direction.

"Is everything recorded on the life chip in our heads?" I ask her.

"Yes, and stored. Why?"

"Well, shouldn't we report the attack on our vehicle the other day? After all, they were Reapers."

164

"I was thinking of reporting it, but I figured it would be better to report everything together, all at once, in the big file I've been preparing about the Revenue Corporation. Once we make this info public and initiate legal action we'll need all the data we can get. If we try to shoot them down prematurely, they'll figure some way to weasel out of it. They always do. Always. We have to go at them with everything we got. Further, there is a high probability they weren't Reapers. There are other forces as at play."

"Yeah, you keep saying that. Why can't we just torture one of those bleached people into confessing? They definitely know what the Revenue Corporation is up to."

She snorts. "Torture? You really *have* been in The Loop! To answer your question – no, we can't do that. Confessions that take place in an entertainment world have no legal validity. They should be, for the same reason someone threatening someone online should be, but this isn't the case. So getting a confession out of one of them wouldn't really do us any good."

Frances lowers into a different airlane. An aeros blazes past, the sound of its honking horn following it.

"Well, in any event, at least we'll have some help in Steam."

"The Assassins?" she asks, flipping the driver the bird.

"Watch it, Tiger!"

"What? Aeros are dangerous vehicles! And don't call me Tiger!"

I laugh, twirling the handle of my cane. If I'm going to be stuck with the damned thing, I might as well get one with a custom blade inside, just like item 139, my swordstick.

"Why are you on edge today? Life ain't too shabby."

"Because we're late, or should I say, *you're late.*"

"Late for what?"

"The agents want to speak with you."

"Husky and Starch again?"

"Quantum, I know you don't listen to me all the time – well ever, really, but seriously, use our lawyer."

I shake my head. "I told you, Frances, I don't like lawyers."

~*~

Agents Reynolds and O'Brian have comfortably ensconced themselves in our conference room – *my* conference room – like they're the lord and master of all that they survey. Agent Reynolds has the B-drone performing aerobatics as he studiously ignores Agent O'Brian, who is thoroughly engrossed in the 3-D anime barnyard dwarf porn that his mini-tablet is projecting in front of him, and God, and everybody.

Maybe Reynolds is a nice guy away from his job, but O'Brian is a horrible human being; a vile, disgusting oxygen thief; a criminal misuse of perfectly good protoplasm on so many different levels. What I wouldn't give to be able to deal them a little Loop-based justice. Just thinking about it makes me feel a little bit better, but only a little bit.

"Mr. Hughes," Agent Reynolds says, as he pokes O'Brian, who grunts, sees me, and hastily logs out of his entertainment program.

Agent O'Brian looks like someone melted him down and poured him into last year's dirty clothes. His clip-on tie hangs from the elastic band that almost closes his shirt collar, and if he coughs, sneezes or farts, odds are high he'll blow buttons off of his way-too-tight, speckled-with-food-stains shirt. He's in the same sports jacket he wore last time, only it looks like he's been bunking down at the homeless shelter in it since then. Before I even sit down, I can detect the unmistakable bouquet of the beach at low tide on a hot August afternoon during kelp and octopus season wafting gently from him. The only thing he lacks to render the whole effect complete is a halo of flies to dog fight with the B-drone.

I can only hope he finds my combination of *Sweaty Haptic Ultra-Funk* and *Baja Mountain Estrus* equally delightful.

I shuffle into my seat with a sour look on my face.

"Mr. Hughes," Agent Reynolds says. He casually gestures to the B-drone now hovering behind them. "Be advised that while this is not a sworn official statement, this conversation is being recorded."

My tongue presses against the inside of my cheek.

"Use up all your smart alecky remarks last time? Not going to say nothing?" O'Brian asks.

"This is just a friendly conversation, not an interrogation," Agent Reynolds says. "We just need a little more information and some clarification here and there. This is all ... off the record."

If you're recording it, it's not off the record – I almost say it, but I keep my mouth shut instead. Besides, Frances has promised me pancakes and beer if I play nice.

"We'd just like you to clear up a few questions we have about what went down at the Long-Term Coma Care Facility." Agent Reynolds says.

I shrug, make the *I dunno* face.

"You are correct," Agent O'Brian says, his eyebrows lowering. "You aren't required to speak to us. However, not speaking to us does not improve your position, and forces us to draw some unflattering conclusions about your veracity and your role in Mr. MacAfee's unfortunate demise."

"Cut the crap," I say, ripping my vow of silence to shreds. "I don't have to speak to you and I'm doing so voluntarily. If you continue this harassment, I'll get an attorney. It's as simple as that. Now, may I go?"

"We just want to … "

"You already know what happened. Reapers from the Revenue Corporation attacked me," I say, my voice raising. "If it hadn't been for Frances Euphoria, and some quick thinking on my part – thank you very much – they would have killed me. They threatened and assaulted me in the virtual world I was trapped in, too."

"Alleged threats and assaults made in virtual worlds are not actionable in the real … " Agent O'Brian starts to say.

"You want my statement or not?" I tell him, pushing back from the table. My cane falls, my back twinges and I grimace.

"Not such a tough guy in the real world, are you Mr. Hughes?" he asks.

168

"Listen you … " He's hoping I'll say something like, *well, I was tough enough to kill that guy in the vat, wasn't I?* and I bite my lip because I really do want to. Instead, I say "I was trying to keep the guy that tried to drown *me* from having another go at it when he un-stunned. Too bad, so sad that he inadvertently drowned, but at most – *at most* – all you got is lawful self-defense. Even more than that, the video record from the coma ward corroborates this! And how do I know about the video record? I was visited by a couple of actual detectives from the Cincinnati PD, and they showed it to me – that's how! Now why don't you two Keystone Kops quit wasting my time, get the video from the Cincinnati PD and get after the *real* bad guys?"

"I don't know what you think you saw, Mr. Hughes, but there is no video record." Agent Reynolds blandly states, "The facility's server malfunctioned just after the incident and corrupted all the video log files before the police could obtain copies."

"Then what did they show me? Don't you even try to pull the old eighteen-and-a-half-minute gap trick on me, you obfuscating, fascist bastards!" I shout. I realize that that little outburst probably just cost me my pancakes, but boy, did it ever feel good!

Agent O'Brian jots something down. His smart-ass grin has morphed into something orc-like and threatening. I have the notion to reach across the table and give him the Moe Howard *eye-poke, nose-twist, hair-pull.*

A knock at the door startles all three of us. Frances enters with coffee for the agents, looks at me, rolls her eyes and shakes her head.

"We were unaware that a copy of the video allegedly survived," Agent Reynolds says after she's left. He straightens his tie, glances at his superior. "Do you have the contact info for the detectives who you claim showed you a video recording of the incident?"

169

"As a matter of fact, I don't," I say, still glaring O'Brian down. "Are we done here, gentlemen? I have actual work to do."

~\*~

Frances already had pancakes on hand before I ever sat down with the F-BIIGie Piggies, but she very pointedly put the beer back in the fridge. Well, you can't always get what you want, and with a full tummy and the premises rendered swine-free, I'm feeling a little better about going back to Steam to do what I do best. Still, I'm a little troubled by the agents and their claims. What's their angle? What are they trying to get at? If they're anything like the agents I've encountered in The Loop, they're in someone's pocket, maybe even the RevCo itself.

Leave the real world be – from one dive to another.

Floating in a vat at the Dream Team Headquarters on my way to a virtual world. I listen as Rocket busies himself with Frances' rig as I relax further into my own vat, feeling the gel around my body. Dive suits are waterproof, but the stuff they have us in isn't exactly water. The specialized silicone substance is mainly for conducting electricity, as vats promise the best in full immersion, meaning that even the smallest sensation can be felt. This differs from the haptic chair back at my hotel.

"I'm going to have the two of you spawn as closely to Ray Steampunk's airship as possible," Rocket says.

"Can't you just put us on the airship?" I ask.

"I'm afraid it's not that simple. I could, however, put you on Clockpunch Mountain, which sits beneath the airship, on the other side. Then you could take the cable car to the top."

"I'm not too keen on that cable car," I say. "Bad experience last time. What about those jetpacks that the Reapers had? Can you get some of those?"

"I'm sure your weapons dealer friend can get you some. You know, the one who sold you the Slice Bang."

Steampunk Santa Claus with the elaborate weapon cache beneath his main salesroom – he also sold Frances and me the Steam Packs, which definitely are worth the price of admission.

"Fine, send us there."

"Don't forget to take your potions as soon as you spawn. It will help a little, at least while you're in Locus."

# Chapter Thirteen

Reality splice – cut to the now. Feedback an answer, an anathema, an algorithmic moment of bliss. My hands materialize in front of me and fingerless gloves appear. The gears for my wrist gun crank, signaling they're ready. As soon as I'm able, I down item 563, the player indicator potion. From there, I equip my Steam Pack, item 564, and the aforementioned wrist gun just in case. The nozzle of my Steam Pack sinks into the port on my arm and my life bar brightens.

Frances Euphoria is clad in what I can only describe as a leather bathing suit with straps that cross behind her neck. The bottom of the bathing suit rounds off into a pair of ultra-tight boy shorts and a pair of thigh-high snakeskin boots

"Seriously, Rocket?" Frances asks, looking up at the sky as if she were speaking to God.

Rocket: I'm just trying to make the two of you blend in.

"Good work," I tell him.

Frances chugs her potion and the indicator turns green. With the snap of her fingers, her hair becomes red again. Her finger comes up and her Shoulder Rocket appears.

"You and your red hair … "

"A girl likes what a girl likes."

"Why don't you have red hair in the real world?"

"Some fantasies are best kept under lock and key," she says, twirling a pretend key.

"Right … "

The boy is selling newspapers in the same spot as yesterday, on the opposite side of a fountain. A small crowd of freaks and geeks has gathered around him, all in unnecessarily bulky gear. A Charles Laughton Quasimodo shuffles past us, his prosthetic leg crafted from rusted metal and pistons.

"Reapers have joined the Boilerplate Army in Morlock!" the newsie calls out. "Reapers have joined the Boilerplate Army in Morlock! Read all about it!"

"Do you think Strata Godsick is there?" I ask Frances.

Rocket answers for her, his dialogue appearing beneath my life bar.

Rocket: There's no way to tell unless you go to the battle. Steam doesn't have a monitoring system like some of the other worlds, meaning I can't tap into a local feed somewhere.

"Thanks, have you seen him in person?" I ask Frances. "Strata Godsick?"

Her eyebrows draw together. "I met him back when you rescued me in 2050 … "

"I can hardly remember any of that," I admit.

"Digital coma for eight years … "

"Two years … "

"You are horrible at math," she says. "You yourself counted five hundred fifty days. That's hardly two years."

173

"Close enough. Back to Strata. Have you ever seen him in a Proxima World? Does he ever lead the Reaper assaults?"

"No idea. Not many have seen him since about 2054. He is hyper reclusive."

"Do he's probably not at the battle then."

The fact that I hardly remember him doesn't have any effect on the knowledge of what he has done. I know he's been killing people in Proxima Worlds to collect insurance money; I know he sent people after me, both in VE dreamworlds and the real world; I know he tried to coerce me into joining his side, and that he tried to have me kidnapped or killed back in the digital coma ward.

"We'll have to deal with Strata later," she says as she registers the look on my face. "If there is anyone who can bring him out of his hole, it's *you*."

My inventory list comes up and I access Dolly's Seed, item 556.

A glimmering oval appears in the air before me.

"Ever used one of these things before?" I ask her. Light radiates from the seed; a tiny galaxy of stars spirals around it.

"Not ever. Never even seen one before."

Frances takes a step closer to examine it. "It sure is pretty, like something that should be in a museum or around a queen's neck."

"Maybe I'm supposed to touch it … "

One press and the seed shatters into a million glittery pixels.

I look up at the two moons over Locus, hoping to see Dolly or Aiden appear in a portal or a chariot of fire or something. The only thing above us is a zeppelin and a thin fog.

"Is that it?" Frances asks.

"Maybe I did it wrong."

"So this is Steam? Interesting!" I turn to find Morning Assassin, decked out in his usual duds. I can tell he's grinning even with the balaclava on his face. My Slice Bang is in his hand, the blade facing towards the pavement.

"Aiden! Where's Dolly?"

"Here." Dolly steps out of a slit in the air like a queen surveying a lesser realm. Her hair bounces as she walks towards me.

~*~

"How do you want to look?" Dolly asks Aiden.

"Ummm ... "

He glances at some of the people gathered around the newsstand. "Okay, I'd like my left arm to have some sort of Gatling gun attached to it." His arm morphs. "I'd also like to be wearing a mask, something that covers the lower half of my face. No! I always wear a mask. I want something like a turtle neck, but over-sized, up to here." He taps his hand at the bottom of his chin. "Great big goggles please, like aviator goggles only bigger, reflective red lenses, and tiny windshield wipers. For my clothing, I'd like to wear what Quantum is wearing: a cutaway jacket with tails – maroon please, big golden hairbrush epaulets, lots of gold braid and two rows of big brass buttons down the front. – and black flared hip breeches with rawhide reinforcements, big pirate boots with brass buckles and silver spurs that jingle-jangle-jingle, and a top hat with a .44 caliber LeMat Revolver mounted inside. Oh, and fingerless gloves."

"Get your own style," I tell him with a grin.

"I thought that this was *everybody's* style here." He grins back.

"Touché."

Aiden looks down at his new Gatling gun. "Can you add a retractable blade to my arm? Make it three. Shoot straight out, then forms something I can twist."

Dolly nods and Aiden's arm rearranges itself. He flicks his arm down and a single blade, as thick as a katana, shoots out. With the twist of his wrist, it separates into pieces, forming something that would do Wolverine justice. He takes a few slices at the air, his copy of my Slice Bang in his right hand and the blades in his left, becoming used to the weight.

"Damn, Aiden," I tell him. "I may need to get me one of those. Talk about Ginsu knives!"

Dolly's eyes flash as she takes in Frances Euphoria's appearance. I can't quite tell what she's thinking – if she's thinking – but I do sense something.

A bolero jacket appears on the NVA Seed's body. This is followed by a corset which tightens until her breastesses nearly pop out the top. The bottom of her corset mutates into a tiny skirt and a pair of high-heeled boots appears on her feet. She does one turn to show me her outfit; I catch her ass cheeks peeking out the bottom of her skirt.

"It's a little short ... "

The skirt elongates an inch. "Better?"

"No complaints here. Aiden?"

"I'm sorry, what now? I was mesmerized by Dolly's accoutrements."

Dolly smiles and winks, "Never heard of them called *accoutrements* before."

"Rocket?"

Rocket: I took some screenshots, if you don't mind.

"Thanks, Rocket. And yes, I *do* mind. I'd better not catch you ... "

Aiden says. "Is Rocket your monitor?"

"Bingo."

Frances clears her throat. "We really need to get a move on, especially if Reapers are now fighting alongside the Boilerplate Army."

"Right, jetpacks. Oh, and weapons. Did you get the weapons made?" I ask Aiden.

"Yes, an Almost Universal Solvent Hose Gun, at your service."

The weapon appears. I add it to my inventory list, item 566. It looks like it came out of the Pope's Fancy Fitments for Renaissance Cathedrals workshop and not something Dirty Dave threw together from whatever crap he had on hand. When I say so, Dolly smiles, says "Well, I did help him out a little bit with materials."

If Bryanboy had owned a World War Two flamethrower, this is exactly what it would have looked like. The two highly polished chrome plated tanks that hold the separate components of the Almost Universal Solvent are lavishly engraved in a traditional oak and ivy style. They are mounted side-by-side on a rococo backpack frame of wrought aluminum openwork, with butter-soft padded leather straps and golden buckles. The smaller pressure tank is also beautifully chromed and engraved, and nestles between the twin component tanks. Polished brass and copper tubing connects the pressure tank to the two component tanks; a silken hose reinforced with woven gold wire runs from each component tank to the solid gold mixing chamber and spray wand, which is set off with carved amber and ivory grips.

A particularly nice touch is the Lawyer's warning on the spray wand, engraved in Blackadder script: *WARNING! Before use, read safety warnings and principles of operation in Operator's Manual, available free of charge from Dirty Dave's Mayhem Mart. For best results, only use genuine Dirty Dave's Chemical Components. Dirty Dave cannot be held responsible for end user's actions.*

"I added a little hack to it as well," Dolly says. "The chemicals will never run out and the pressure tank is always full."

"Very nice. You *do* know what a boy likes."

Aiden turns to Frances. "I had something made for you as well."

"You did?" She cuts me down with a dirty look. "How sweet … and here I thought I'd been forgotten."

"How could you ever think that?" Aiden approaches her and takes her wrist. "I figured some type of wrist attachment that sprayed the AUS may be helpful to you."

178

"That's so sweet, so thoughtful!"

He places a device on her wrist. From there, he attaches a portion to her forearm and a trigger comes down into her palm. " ... and it's solid gold! Just press the button," he says, making direct eye contact with her.

*Is Aiden ... ?* I cast the thought away. There's no way he's flirting with Frances, the sly dog.

"So we have weapons; now we need jetpacks," I say, cutting their moment short. "You can't just make these appear, can you?" I ask Dolly.

She smiles again, "I am an entity of many talents; check your inventory lists."

~*~

In the air above Locus.

Dolly zips in front of me and her skirt flaps in the wind, giving me a fairly nice view. A black and orange tiger-striped triplane approaches and I bank left to intercept. I hang about an aircraft's length off his wings, and the pilot – a human player in a leather propeller beanie and aviator goggles – glares at me, ostentatiously charges his machine guns, and dives away as I pass.

Aiden whooshes in front of me, his arms at his sides. He twists right, and cuts through a cloud of steamy exhaust coming from a zeppelin overhead. I arc upwards, until I'm just inches away from the whale-shaped craft. Slowing, I run my fingers along its side to feel the texture.

179

I glance down and take in the world that is Steam, the city of Locus. From my vantage point, I can see that the city is actually laid out in a copy/pasted grid. The uniqueness of the city lies in how people have modified the buildings. Other than that, it falls into a pattern of three square plots, a rectangle plot and four triangle plots followed by a power plant.

Advancing towards Ray Steampunk's airship, I laugh out loud at what my life has become, how free it is while I'm in the air. The feeling is exhilarating; the spinning world only reminds me of how closely all worlds are related, be they of neuronal or material construction – the threads of life blur at top speeds.

A steam missile whistles past, ending my brief reverie.

Rocket: Air Enforcers incoming one o'clock!

Moments later, I'm on a pair of human players in wasp-like costumes and canvas wings. The two pick up their pace, jockeying for a position of advantage.

The one I didn't see collides with me from behind, wraps her arms around me, folds her wings and we drop like a stone. I swing elbows behind me – left, right, left – and she anticipates right again and dodges left, I connect with my left elbow and really ring her dinner bell. She goes limp; I twist in her embrace and put her out of the game with my wrist gun. She flutters to earth like a broken butterfly, trailing steam.

I push hard to regain altitude and aim for the Air Enforcer chasing Frances, but she deals with him before I get close. She rolls onto her back, points Aiden's gift at him, and unleashes a cloud of AUS. The Air enforcer is too close to avoid it and he flies right into it; almost immediately his wing fabric dissolves and he explodes into steam. His screams cut off abruptly as he logs out, the chickenshit bastard quitter.

The *pop-pop-pop* of weapons fire draws my attention. Aiden's the center of a whirling furball of five or six Air Enforcers. He's firing short bursts with his arm Gatling and manipulating the *slice* part of his Slice Bang like Inigo Montoya with Edward Scissorhands ... hands. He's put three down just in the time it takes for me to notice him, and looks to be having more fun than a catnip basket full of double-pawed kittens on nitrous oxide.

I move to go help.

And promptly get blindsided *again* because I failed to pay attention *again*. This Air Enforcer is bigger than I am, and he drives me up against the zeppelin I'd been recently admiring, knocks the wind out of me and promptly tries to skewer my giblets with a triple-bladed Wolverine claw set-up. He's got me pinned face first against the fabric of the airship and I'm expecting to get fileted in the next two or three heartbeats.

His head comes off and spins away; steam gouts from his neck stump and his body slides away from me. Aiden hovers there, touches the brim of his top hat with the blade of his Slice Bang, grins like a madman and jets off.

I almost feel bad about all the unpleasant ways I offed him all those times.

The tiger-striped triplane chases Dolly as it spits long streamers of tracer at her. She twists and dodges, flips and rolls, loops under and then comes up alongside the plane, plucks the pilot out and throws him. His sissy scream dopplers away and abruptly cuts off when he logs out and disappears; his orphaned propeller beanie makes a controlled descent, and the unpiloted triplane goes into a flat spin and plummets away.

181

A pair of Air Enforcers dart in to intercept her; she turns, and in the classic *Supergirl in flight* pose, flies *right through them*, bursting them like extra-festive piñatas filled with sparkly digital confetti.

And just like that, the sky is clear of winged foe. We hover and huddle up like a high school rollerball squad just about to go in for the second half.

"Is everybody okay?" Aiden asks. He appears particularly solicitous of Frances, who's got a slight scratch that's spitting a little steam. She actually *simpers*, giggles, and twirls her hair around her finger as he examines her owie. I look at Dolly, and she gives me the raised eyebrows and shoulder shrug.

Rocket: Your immediate airspace is clear for the next few minutes, but there are hostile forces en route from three directions. Recommend that you move, now.

"Thanks, Big R, we're outta here." I reply. Aiden and Frances are like a pair of middle schoolers and oblivious to their surroundings – says the guy who got blindsided twice because *he* wasn't paying attention during aerial combat. I snap my fingers to get their attention, "Yo, Suzy, Sam – bad guys on the way, we gots to vamoose now.

"Let's go!" Dolly says, zipping ahead.

The four of us speed higher into the sky. Locus shrinks below us and I can see the slopes of Clockpunch Mountain. The cable car is about two-thirds of the way up to the landing stage and filled with tourists and pilgrims to the fount of all that is Steam. I hover alongside like a hummingbird of unusual size in outlandish Edwardian glad rags, and the looky-loos all point and exclaim and *ooh* and *ahh*. I watch the magic metallic chicken legs as they pedal away, and I land on the platform beside the garish Easter egg tank.

The NPC conductor throws the front door open, shouts, "Oi! No free rides! Where's your ... erm ... " and trails off as he looks down the wrong end of my arm roscoe.

"Back inside, Ringo. Keep the cash customers calm and nobody gets hurt."

The dump valve for the Easter egg tank is an impossible-to-miss red hand wheel the size of a trash can lid marked *Do Not Open When Carriage is in Motion!* I open it, steam spurts out the bottom of the tank, the legs stop pedaling and the carriage ceases its motion.

Several of the stupider passengers do the *scream for no reason when something unexpected happens* as I jet away, and I'm sore tempted to go back and demonstrate a little ballistic Darwinism on them. Several of the *really stupid* passengers lean out the windows and blaze away at me. So much for trying to be a kinder, gentler Quantum – I should have cut the cable and killed them all in the first place like I'd usually do.

FE Hangs back, waits for me to pull alongside her, "What was that all about? I thought we were in a hurry!"

"Tactics, my good Euphoria, tactics. Remember what happened when they outed us as Reapers the first time?"

"Y-e-e-s-s-s. Most of them ran away or logged out."

"Yeah, but some chose to stand and fight, and we're going to have enough going on without additional unfriendly guns at our back."

"I'm surprised that you just didn't blow up the cable car or have your usual slaughterfest or something," she observes, with just the slightest hint of snark.

183

This on top of the knuckleheads in the cable car popping off at me after I *didn't* kill them is not bolstering my self-esteem nor assuaging my inner child. I let go with a deep, heartfelt sigh. "Yeah, sorry about that; I'll make sure to kill extra next time to make up for it." She gives me a look, says nothing, jets off to fly alongside Aiden.

Women; can't live with 'em, can't shoot 'em.

~*~

We hit the flight deck and I equip everything I can possibly carry. My Steam Pack stays on, jet pack over that, the Hose Gun goes on in front, the wrist gun stays on and I jam my saber pistol under my belt.

"Got enough gear?" Frances asks me in that *almost but not quite* snarky tone.

"Better to have a gun and not need it than to need a gun and not have it, sister."

The deck of the airship ripples and quakes. On the other side of the landing field, the two Transformer-sized Steam Enforcers have come alive, and they've brought a few friends.

Air Enforcers explode towards us like a swarm of rabid, rocket-propelled killer butterflies. Aiden is already airborne, and laughs as he rises to meet them.

"Cover Aiden!" I shout to Frances. "Dolly and I will take the Steam Enforcers!"

Frances lifts into the air on a column of steam and sprouts a Gatling gun arm of her own. She and Aiden hover side-by-side and put out a river of fire to keep the Air Enforcers away from Dolly and me.

The Steam enforcers are bigger that I remember them being – they're tremendous, gigantic, *Ghostbusters Stay Puft Marshmallow Man* huge, *Bibendum* made metallic on a Godzilla scale; They're stinkin' big!

I goose my jetpack and activate my advanced abilities. An Air Enforcer gets past Aiden and Frances and makes for me in slow motion; I have all the time in the virtual world to draw my saber pistol and present it so he skewers himself. He logs out and vanishes, unsticking the blade before I have to fire the pistol.

The Steam Enforcer swings to swat me like a mosquito; I dodge easily and catch a time-dilated glimpse of Dolly as she hovers in front of Great Big Steam Guy Number Two, eyes ablaze with orange fire. Glittering articulated appendages of chainsaw blades and metallic shark's teeth erupt from her back like the chains from Lemarchand's box.

If this is what she used on Rollins when she stood him off while I logged out from the Loop that first time, it's no wonder he screamed like a little girlie-girl. I'm anxious to see the fullness of this transformation, but now ain't the time.

*She's fine! Keep your eye on the prize!* says the voice in my head, as I jet over my big metal friend, dodge another swat, and get a good look at its back. It's got a steam pack just like mine, if mine was the size of a UPX delivery aeros.

That's why nothing touched it in our first little dust-up; it all makes sense, or as much sense as anything does in this crazy, clunky, faux-retro Steam world.

*Cut the steam, cut the power, cut the giant down to size!*

185

Well, no duh, little voice.

I flip the ivory rocker switch on the golden Almost Universal Solvent wand and the system gurgles as it pressurizes; flick the safety forward in the trigger guard, finger on the trigger and I hose the giant steam pack down with Dirty Dave's finest Alchemic Unpleasantness.

The results are most gratifying.

The Steam Enforcer melts away like a snowman in a golden shower; the damaged steam pack blasts out tremendous gouts of high pressure steam as it dissolves. Just to really spoil its day, I give its innards a good big squirt through the widening hole where the steam pack used to be.

The Steam Enforcer locks up, wobbles, crashes face down into the deck with a cosmic KABOOM, and sends visible ripples throughout the fabric of the airship. There's a last burst of firing, and I hear Frances holler, "Aiden, no! Don't pursue, let them run!"

Dolly is perched atop a humongous mound of shredded metal and broken gears, her Doc Ock accoutrements nowhere in evidence. She nonchalantly buffs her nails and then critically examines the results. I know that she's doing it strictly for show, but *Dang* that gal has style. She catches my eye, gives me a coquettish grin, and daintily picks her way down from atop the heap of former Steam Enforcer.

~*~

Aiden lands next to me. "That was great! Can we go again, daddy? Can we?" His grin is all teeth and fierce shining eyes, and despite our growing bromance, still makes me feel like a three-legged arthritic deer at the wolf pack potluck supper when the casseroles run out.

The big F.E. lands next, fine as ever in her steampunk attire. She gives Dolly a pointedly neutral look, gives me a look that's considerably less neutral, and takes Aiden's arm as she gushes, "Oh Aiden, you were great! You got so many that I hardly had to shoot."

Seriously? No lecture on algorithmic brutality, or 'NPCs are people too', or 'you've been in The Loop too long? Sheesh!'

He blushes, and she turns to Dolly and me, "Now we get to Ray."

"Got any idea of what we should ask him?"

I put eyeballs on *Schloss Schteampünken.* The gothic revival-style castle is directly across from us at the far end of the airfield. It's gaudy and kitschy and I suspect that the lavish entrance is mainly for show – just a backdrop for the tourists' souvenir postcards. The guts, the important bits, the *Sanctum Sanctorum* are obviously below.

Rocket: Ray Steampunk was one of the last people to see Strata Godsick before he disappeared. He may know something we can use as leverage. Tell him who you are and who you work for.

"Thanks, Peanut Gallery." My eyes move from Rocket's message to my life bar, which is pulsating blue. My advanced abilities bar is pretty much nil, but the brightened ring around it has started to replenish.

A hand squeezes mine; it's Dolly.

"Good job, Doll," I tell her, as everything else around me fades into insignificance and I focus exclusively on her.

"You too." His smile illuminates her from within, and my heartbeat picks up just that little bit more.

"You have to show me that trick sometime, you know, those things that grow out of your back. I always seem to be busy when you do it."

She bites her lip. "It's not exactly attractive; it's definitely not how I want you to think of me."

"Are you two finished?" Frances asks, stepping in front of me, hands on hips.

"Almost." I take Dolly's hand in both of mine, and in a simpering falsetto say, "Oh Dolly, you were great! You crunched up so many I hardly had to melt any!"

Frances' eyes narrow, Dolly barely suppresses a mirthful nose-snort.

"Now then, you were saying … ?"

"Hey, I'd just like to get this assignment wrapped up so I … so *we* can move on to something else." And she huffs off.

The four of us jetpack over the barbican that separates the castle from the airfield. The castle itself looks like a rusty, stylized, cast iron copy of *Neuschwanstein* with all the magic and fairytale cuteness hammered out of it. Onion domes shingled with tarnished scales of copper and silver and bronze top the various towers. Girning, post-industrial gargoyles spout plumes of steam at irregular intervals.

188

"Do you think he went a little overboard?" I tap the end of my Slice Bang against a bollard of whirring gears that spit steam. "Just a little?"

Aiden says, "It isn't going to be easy getting through that door."

The only entrance is an arch, sealed by a massive, metal, Steam Enforcer-sized door that's covered with Industrial Revolution bas-reliefs; there's no corresponding cat-flap for us less heroically proportioned peons. A huge bust of James Watt gazes down upon us from a plinth atop the arch. In a surprisingly indecorous decorative touch, steam fizzles from his ears. Frances Euphoria sends her weapons back to inventory and approaches the door unarmed.

"Careful," I call over to her. "It may be booby-trapped."

She ignores me and knocks twice. The sound is reverberant, huge. If he's in there, he's sure to have heard it.

I activate my jetpack and steam my way over to the door. I throw a few pirouettes in as I fly, just because. Sure, I could walk, but jetpacking is just so excellent! I land next to Frances and hammer on the door with the butt of the Slice Bang. "Hey Steampunk, open the door in the name of the law, you bastard!" I shout. "We know you're in there!"

Frances looks at me, rolls her eyes and shakes her head. "Really? *Really?* That's how you're going to start a conversation?"

"Well," I tell her under my breath, "he *is* a bastard. Only a bastard would make a steampunk world with so many damned rules and live in an airship above the place in Olympian splendor like some sort of God made flesh. Just saying."

"I have to agree with Quantum." Aiden says.

189

"What's the problem?" Dolly asks. "The only thing the Almost Universal Solvent won't dissolve is gold; that door's not gold, so dissolve us an entrance if you want in, Mr. Hughes."

"That's not a bad idea, Doll."

I give the door the old *your name in the snow* treatment with my superior golden wand. The AUS works like … well, *magic* and dissolves a whopping great hole in the door – and the floor underneath. A half-turn of the nozzle and I get mist instead of a heavy stream. I melt us a nice round hole in the door about ten feet away from my first attempt, without damaging the floor as much.

"Watch out going through," says I. "You probably don't want to get any of that stuff on you."

~*~

The huge circular foyer is empty aside from a low pentagrammatic platform; a single shaft of light illuminates the large golden speaking tube exactly in the star's center. A tremendous gear and crystal chandelier is suspended from the vaulted ceiling high above us and doesn't provide much illumination nor dispel the shadows in the distance. Our footsteps echo and rebound; the whole place feels like a trap, an ambush.

Aiden says, "I'll check for another way out," as he engages his stealth mode and becomes dim and insubstantial.

"The speaking tube's the only thing in here; that's gotta be it." Frances Euphoria walks steps up to the platform, and as she enters the beam of light, nothing happens.

I ready *everything* just in case.

"It's a speaking tube; I'll speak to it and see what happens. She leans over it in that legs straight, bend from the waist with the back arched pin-up pose and brushes a strand of hair out of her face. "Ummm … hello?"

*"HELLO."*

The voice comes from the corners of the room, loud and booming. Frances' eyes dart from Dolly to me.

"Go on," I tell her.

"We are here to see Ray Steampunk," she says.

*"RAY STEAMPUNK?"*

The thunderous voice causes digital dust to fall from the ceiling.

"Yes," she says into the pipe, "Ray Steampunk."

*"WHAT DO YOU WANT WITH RAY STEAMPUNK?"*

"We are members of the DREAM Team – Dream Recovery Extraction and Management Team funded by the FCG."

*"THE DREAM TEAM?"*

"Yes."

*"SILLY NAME."*

191

"See, I told you." I scoot in next to Frances and lean over the golden pipe, placing my hand over the opening.

"You're the one who came up with the name," she whispers.

"I'm pretty sure that was Godsick."

"I thought you forgot everything," she says.

"We can discuss this later." I remove my hand from the pipe opening and say, "Quit being such a reclusive little shitbird and come out here and talk to us already, Ray." Frances hits me and I continue. "We're here for very important reasons, and we don't have all day."

The floor rattles and hums and the sound of cranking gears fills the room. Aiden appears on my right, and Dolly isn't far behind.

The platform smoothly drops below floor level, descending around the speaking tube which remains in place like a fixed spindle.

"Weapons up, face outward, stay frosty," I say aloud. "Who knows what will happen next."

# Chapter Fourteen

The platform grinds to a halt; a tiny, star-shaped patch of illumination high above us shows just how far we've descended. A portion of the wall slides open; Aiden goes first, his Gatling gun arm leads. Frances follows him in with her retro submachine gun; Dolly puts her hand on my shoulder. "You next," she whispers, "I'll cover our back trail." We move through a hallway now, the walls of which are adorned with oil paintings of generals in ornate blue or gray uniforms, generals in red coats and white helmets, generals in field gray and spiked Prussian helmets. There are wall-mounted candles every yard or so, and the hallway is defined by teardrop shaped pools of light.

"Rocket, where are we?"

Rocket: In-game GPS has been disabled. You're likely in the airship somewhere, or you've been teleported somewhere else …

Aiden turns to me to say something. His mouth opens, but no words come out.

"What?" I ask.

He tries to speak again, and again nada.

"Dolly?"

She puts her hand over her mouth and shakes her head no; points to her ears and gives a thumbs up.

I turn to Frances. "What's gotten into them?"

193

Frances says, "I don't have a clue – I've never seen this before."

"Are you guys okay otherwise?" I ask, and get a thumbs up from them both. "Might as well press on."

The hallway brightens with each step forward, as if the sun were resting at its end, waiting to blind us. As soon as I breach the threshold of the door, my life bar drops to a quarter full and my advanced abilities bar disappears completely.

"WELCOME."

~*~

I size up His Lordship and I'm not impressed.

Ray Steampunk's throne is deliberately designed to astonish and confound; to overawe and convey the very quintessential steampunkyness of his whole extravaganza. I'm at the point now where I'm all *Oh, look Honey! It's yet another damn thing made of whirling gears and rusted metal and pipes that spouts steam!*

Gimme a frickin' break – seriously.

His most Serene and Majestic Steaminess is garbed in gilded armor with a string of gears and dials and gauges across the front of his chest. His left arm is completely mechanical, accented with polished silver, the hand of which ends in an ornate leather gauntlet. A golden indicator above his head signifies that he is much, much more than just another player. His eyes are pressed shut, as if he's meditating.

"Ready to talk, Your Highness?" I ask the Geared and Gilded Goomba.

"Mr. Steampunk," says Frances as she puts the elbow in my short ribs, "we apologize for this intrusion, but it's of the utmost importance that we talk with you."

"So it would seem. Yours was a most direct and unusual approach of which I most highly disapprove. However, you are here now, so state your business." I can hear his voice coming from him, but I've yet to see his lips move. Perks of being a developer I suppose.

"How about we cut the small talk and get down to business, Ray?"

Dolly tugs on my sleeve, points to Steampunk with an open hand, then puts that hand on her chest and nods *yes*. She points to Steampunk again, puts her hand on my chest and shakes her head *no.*

"Yeah, he's the NVA Seed like you and not just a player like me – I get it, Doll."

She silently sighs, puts her face in her hand like she's got a headache.

"What is it then?" Not quite so quietly this time.

"Enough," Steampunk says.

"We've come to speak with you about Strata Godsick," diplomat Frances says. "You were his last known contact."

"Was I indeed?"

"Yes, sir. We want info about Strata Godsick," Frances says, "whatever you can tell us. You know about his illegal and unethical activities. His Reapers kill people in Proxima Worlds; the people they kill there also really die in the real world, and his corporation collects their insurance money. Further, he's imprisoned and enslaved hundreds upon hundreds of people in various Proxima Worlds and uses them as his cannon fodder. If a human player kills them, they die in real life. We have to stop to this."

"This is none of my concern," he says.

"What?" I demand, fists clenched. "Are you truly so distanced and disconnected here in your fantasy dream world? Real deaths in the real world mean nothing to you?"

"No. Why should they? Would my death mean anything to *them*?"

Frances says, "Please, Mr. Steampunk. Information. That's all we're asking for."

He thinks for a moment. "I will give you the information you seek, but you must first resolve an issue that requires immediate attention."

"As long as it doesn't involve grails or broomsticks."

He ignores me and continues, "The Reapers have aligned themselves with the Boilerplate Army–"

"–See! It does concern you."

He opens his eyes – cold eyes, dead eyes, round, black soulless doll's eyes – and locks me in his gaze. I don't want to, but I look away first.

"I am unconcerned about the Reapers per se. It is their alliance with the Boilerplate Army that disconcerts me, and the metastasizing chaos and destruction they have unleashed upon my realm. Left unchecked, it will destroy all that I have wrought here, and I will not have that. I want this war to end."

"Oh c'mon – *you're* the Head Honcho, The Big Cheese, The Deus ex Machina – can't you just work a little algorithmic magic with the ones and zeroes and fix your problem right up, Your Most Pluperfect Retro-Techness? Ow! Dammit, Frances!"

Frances pinched me, *hard.* Just like my … just like my mother used to do when she thought I was acting the fool.

"It is my policy to act as *the man behind the curtain* rather than as the visible Hand of God, save in direst need. It is less disruptive, and provides a better experience for the participants. I prefer more subtle and mundane interventions."

Frances snorts at *subtle.*

"Ah, I got it. You want *us* to fight."

"No, I want you to resolve an issue in exchange for the information you seek. If you choose not to do so, log out now and you will be blocked from re-entering my domain."

Rocket: The man can bargain.

"I can see that," I say under my breath.

"We'll do it – we agree!" Frances says.

"Very well," says His Most Awesome Rattle-and-Clankness. "I have gifts you will find useful. Equip your mutant hacks and approach me."

Frances' arm morphs into her giant double barrel shootin' iron; I access the golden ax and it melts up my arm and forms my Blast-O-Matic.

*Hello Quantum.*

Not now, little voice in my head – busy.

We stand before His August Majesty, and Himself leans forward and touches a fingertip to the muzzle of our weapons. There's a flash behind my eyes, my mouth tastes metallic, a jolt of lightning juice runs down my spine, and my testicles try to retreat up into my body cavity. My hack gun smokes and steams like it was carved from dry ice.

"I have significantly upgraded your weapons," he intones. "Steam under very high compression draws heat from its surroundings once it is released to expand. *Everything it touches will freeze.*"

I twist my hack, admiring the upgrade. "So it's like a Mr. Freeze gun or something?"

"No, it is an *actual* Mr. Freeze gun – specifically."

"Huh?"

Rocket: Damn … he hooked you up! Freeze something, blast it with the Gramogun and *ZOWIE!* Ever seen a video of an opera singer shattering glass with her voice? That's what you can do now!

"Not bad," I say, examining the ice blue ring around my hack's barrel.

"One last item," says our beneficent host. "Your player status indicators are now golden instead of blue; there are no limitations on your inventory items – you may use any of them without life force penalty. All who see you will know that you are my emissaries."

He snaps his fingers, and my advanced abilities come back on line and my life bar jumps to 250%.

"Prepare yourselves. I will transport you to the battlefields of Morlock … "

# Chapter Fifteen

*... Now.*

We spawn in a wooded area that would induce lachrymal flow in Smokey the Anthropomorphic Ursine. Some of the trees still stand, their bark, branches and foliage stripped away by shellfire. Most have been reduced to stumps and charred fragments and flinders which litter the cratered landscape. The sound of gunfire and explosions reaches my ears, the sky flashes with Iraqi Lightning – we are close.

"This place looks like something out of *Under Fire.*"

"Which is?"

I turn to find Frances Euphoria looking like an angel's cousin with the golden indicator above her head.

"A war book. GoogleFace it." I turn to the Loopers. "Aiden, Dolly, can you speak now?"

Aiden's mouth moves, but no sound comes out.

"Why's Ray still silencing them?" I ask Frances.

"No idea."

Aiden makes the two handed *shooting a machine gun* gesture.

"Can you believe this guy?" I say under my breath to Frances. "This new world has sent him off his rocker."

"I think he wants to borrow one of your machine guns," Frances says.

Aiden points at her and gives her a thumbs up.

"Don't you have your own?" I ask him.

He gestures *machine gun* again.

"Why do you want mine then?"

He rolls his eyes, slaps his forehead with the heel of his hand, makes the *talk-talk-talk* hand puppet gesture and pantomimes *foregrip*, *pistol grip*, and with the tip of his finger draws a big circle in between them to indicate the drum magazine of …

" … the Thompson Submachine Gun. You want the Tommy gun?"

Morning Assassin holds out his hands and makes a very credible *No Duh!* face at me.

The Chicago Typewriter appears in my hands, and though he's too well-mannered to snatch it from me, I know he wants to. He leads us to a reasonably intact wall about fifty paces from where we spawned.

He flips the selector to *semi*, and in a most impressive display of trigger control and rapid-fire exhibition shooting spells out S-T-E-A-M-P-U-N-K in bullet holes.

"Okay," Frances says, "Steampunk … "

He resumes, pauses, resumes, finishes, steps back and admires his work. With a theatrical flourish, he blows the smoke from the muzzle.

The phrase STEAMPUNK IS DEAD is spelled out in bullet holes.

Morning Assassin points at the message on the wall.

"Steampunk is dead ... " Frances says. "Steampunk is dead ... "

"Steampunk ... is dead?" I turn to Dolly. "What's with your button man?"

Aiden pinches me, in the same spot Frances did.

"Ow! Dammit, Aiden – that's gonna leave a mark!" I whine, in a rugged and manly tone.

I step on his foot.

He punches me in the shoulder.

I grab his nose between my pointer and middle finger knuckles and slap that hand down with my other fist. I get the blade hand up over my nose to block, just as he's about to prong two fingers in my eyes.

"Hey you two! Don't make me come over there!" Frances shouts.

Aiden and I both freeze; Dolly shakes with silent laughter.

Frances bounces from foot to foot. "I get it! I get it! In the real world, in *our* world, Ray Steampunk is Dead."

Rocket: He's an RPC? WOWZA!

Aiden gives me two thumbs up. I turn to Dolly and she nods.

"He's ... dead? Like actually dead?"

"Yes! It makes sense now!" Frances looks up the sky. "Rocket, are you getting this?"

Rocket: Mind blown up here, Q! BLOWN! Ray Steampunk is dead, *but* his avatar is still monitoring Steam. His avatar is an NPC, but he's technically an RPC, a Reborn Player Character! This is why we haven't been able to locate Steampunk It all makes sense now! He's remained alive through … through a Proxima World!

"Is that even possible?" I ask.

"It's happened before. Several developers have immortalized themselves in the Proxima Galaxy."

"Why did he silence Dolly and Aiden then?"

"Because they can tell he's an RPC! He doesn't want the world to know; he wants … *his avatar* wants for Ray Steampunk to remain in control as a human player, not an NPC. If word got out, people may turn against him."

I glance at the writing on the wall – *STEAMPUNK IS DEAD* – and start to laugh "So you mean this whole time, this whole time, we've been trying to get in touch with an NPC masquerading as a human – not *Deus Ex Machina* but *Spiritus in Machina*! Crazy!"

Aiden fires the tommy gun in the air like some Middle Eastern knucklehead celebrant. Bad things happen.

~*~

The sky above us rips open and a portal forms, spitting comic book sparks. Reapers spill out, draw their weapons and form a half circle around us. Leather, spikes, skull masks, asshattery, tough guy poses, *Mad Max* extras with more faux muscles than real sense – the murder guild lackeys are a troubled bunch of tweens. Their leader is the last to exit, and plops out like a steaming turd from a dyspeptic pig.

"Rollins," I say, my mutant hack melting up my arm. "I like you better in the tutu, sparkly tiara and fairy wings."

One of his posse guffaws. Rollins sprouts a katana, pivots, and removes the offender's head.

The same fatboy cellar-dweller who took Frances hostage in The Loop stands before me in his partially shattered skull mask and make-believe He-Man avatar. As unlikely as it seems, he's even more bloated and ridiculously proportioned than he was in our previous soirée.

"Ooh, Rollins, what great big arms you have! Can you even reach your pathetic little pee-pee like that?" I ask, and crook my little finger at him.

"Why are you here, Quantum Hughes?"

His arms bulge and ripple as his mutant hacks form, tremendous gun barrels with muzzles like Schwarzenegger sewer pipes.

"You know, I'm going to make it my personal jihad to find you in real life so I can give your flabby ass the spanking your momma never gave you, little boy."

"You are old and weak," he booms in the standard Reaper Vader voder knock-off tones. "A pathetic old man with a cane. I will take it from you, stick it up your ass and spin you around like a propeller! But here, now, prepa-… "

"Say hello to my little friend, fatboy!" The air temperature drops precipitously as the arctic blast envelops him and freezes him mid-threat into a nine foot, quarter-ton stalagmite of very surprised cyber-bully.

His chopper squad scatters and opens up with everything while trying to find cover. Dolly smiles and crosses her arms; all manner of bullets and explode-y projectiles hang motionless in the air in front of us; streamers of flame and energy beams stop dead and dissipate. Morning Assassin gets in amongst them, and becomes the Flying Cuisinart of Death with a Slice Bang in either hand. He laughs like a berserker on crack as he renders Rollins' butt-boy backup band into fugu sashimi.

In the very best kung fu vid tradition, F. E. whirls, twirls, defies gravity and hacks her way through the few B & D Mouseketeers that Aiden hasn't gotten to yet. And then there are none, as the survivors log out like the cowards they are.

Aiden and Frances stop, land, look around, and then sit next to each other, heads together. Dolly stops doing whatever it is she did, and all the formerly flying metal the Reapers fired at us hits the ground with a 'hail on the roof of the aeros' clatter.

My friend Rollins is still here, still frozen solid, and somewhat worse for the wear. He was on the wrong side of Dolly's shield and he's picked up a fair number of chips and dings from misdirected Reaper fire. Because he is thermally inconvenienced and totally immobile, there's no moving the hand to access the log out point for the head Reapercicle. "Okay, Rollins – I have things to do and people to see, so I can't spend as much time on this as I'd like, but it's still going to be darned unpleasant for you."

Item 171, sledge hammer comes up, and I smash his right hand and left hand so there'll be no logging out anytime soon. Both knees and he topples over, both shoulders and his arms come off.

"This is probably going to be wasted effort on my part because I don't think you really have one, but here goes anyway," and I hammer his codpiece into *Extra-Vile Rollins-flavored Slurpee, now with thirty percent more crybaby*. "Once you thaw out enough to log out, you'd better go. You don't want to be here when I come back, or I'll make it really hurt."

Frances comes up behind me. "You have a serious problem."

"How so?" I ask with a smirk. "Revenge is a dish best served cold."

~\*~

Aiden ankles over, cracks his neck, and observes, "What a bunch of big fat chickens!"

"Ummm ... I heard that," I say, looking to Frances.

"I did too."

I turn to Dolly. "You got your singing voice back too?"

Her hand also comes to her throat. "Yes, it appears Ray Steampunk has removed the hack."

"Well, ain't that something."

An explosion in the distance reminds me of our current locale.

Frances says, "We really need to get to the battle."

A sphere of light takes shape between Dolly's fingers. It lifts into the air, growing in size until six forms materialize in the center of the sphere. The UK Assassins. They drop to the ground and Burly is the first to step forward.

"There 'e is!" he says, puffing his chest out. Attached to his back is an AUS weapon similar to mine. While his weapon may be appropriate, his get up isn't. Burly and the rest of the UK Assassins are in their desert camouflage. Bucket Hat is in his namesake and the Quiet Man's face is painted brown with black streaks across his eyes.

"Aye, tis true," Scotty says, "I bloody told ye that we 'ad the wrang gear. If youse arseholes would've only listened … "

Irish Shorty says, "Well, none of us 'ave ever 'eard of steampunk. How are we bloody supposed to dress in a style we're unfamiliar with? Answer me that!"

"You've been full of pish since I met you–"

"What did you say, Pip?" Pip aims his Hose Gun at Scotty.

"Enough bickering," I tell them, "Save that for the real war. Dolly, please give them some world appropriate threads."

Stars and blips of light spiral around the UK Assassins like Tinker Bell at T.J Maxx. Burly is now in a Bane mask and a black tank top with two bandoliers crisscrossing over his chest. Pip is next to him, in a trench coat with a matching top hat and black cowboy boots.

Scotty says, "What do ya think, Quantum?" He does a quick spin, opening his tweed jacket to show me his gray vest with metal spikes along the lapel. Covering his legs and bare *arse* is what only can be described as a steampunk kilt – leather with multiple cargo pockets. His thumb comes up and he winks at me. "*No bad*, eh?"

"You don't want to know what I think."

The Quiet Man is up next, sporting the steampunk-cyborg look in a sleeveless sack coat and old leather stompers. On his face is a leather Mankind mask and there are several grenades strapped to his chest.

"That's a bad place for grenades … "

"Steam grenades," Dolly says, her arm looping in mine.

Irish Shorty has gone for the newsie-cum-assassin look, decked out in tight khakis and a puffy white shirt. Next to him is the Bucket Hat formally known as the Tall One, who would be a spitting image of a young Robert E. Lee if it weren't for the desert camouflage hat still on his head.

"What's with the bucket hat?"

"If ya got a problem with me 'at you can take it up with, King," he shows me his left fist, "William," he shows me his right.

~*~

It doesn't take us long to reach the forward edge of the battle area. The city of Morlock looks like Stalingrad, looks like Dresden, looks like Coventry. There isn't an undamaged building as far as I can see, but there's lots and lots of rubble which means lots and lots of cover for the defenders.

The roar of battle picks up as we approach. Shouts and screams, explosions and Gatling gun fire, the clank and hiss of steam powered war machines combine to create a constant rolling thunder. Fragile looking fantasy aircraft with two or three wings wheel and turn, close and spit fire at each other, separate and dive away. Air Enforcers tangle with the aircraft, with each other, with jet pack equipped flying soldiers, and a genuine crazy woman on a witch's broom swoops low and scatters pink fireballs over the buildings just in front of us. A slather of small arms fire rises to greet her as she makes a second pass, and she suddenly disappears – dead or logged out.

A voice farspeaks us, "Hey, new meat! Over here! Look to your right – the shops with the azaleas in front? Right here." A soldier in a German helmet leans out from around the corner, waves us in, ducks behind the corner. "Don't bunch up as you come across; they've got a spotter somewhere and they're dropping steam rockets on us every chance they get."

A rocket slams into the two story building just behind us and showers us with debris. "Yeah, like that," says the voice. "Cross now, quickly-quickly-quickly."

I'm the last to cross, and the soldier reaches out, grabs my lapel and drags me in front of her as another rocket announces its presence. Shrapnel and debris patter off of her helmet and clamshell body armor.

"Well finally!" she exclaims. "Look at you, Mister and Miz golden indicator and your posse of NPC murderous moppets! The hand of Ray Steampunk made flesh, here to help us out in our hour of need and turn the tide."

208

Her attitude reminds me of me. She also radiates a *don't screw with me* aura that you could cut with a knife. "Yeah, that's us chief. What's going on here?"

"What, all this? It's called *war* and it's here all day, every day. We hold Morlock, and the Boilerplates are hitting us with everything they have, trying to push us out. If they get through us, the way to Locus is open and they've won. They've got three or four Steam Enforcers and a bunch of Air Enforcers, and these frickin' road warrior lookin' dudes who use banned weapons and cheat like crazy bastards."

She spits a stream of digital tobacco juice and continues.

"I'm trying to keep their attention focused here so I can get some of my troops in to hit 'em on the flank and roll up their line. If we can do that, *we've* won. But those big-ass Steam Enforcers are killing us, and most of my knuckleheads just want to run around, yell and scream, shoot guns and blow shit up. They die and respawn and die and respawn, but they're not really doing us any good. If we can take down the Steam Enforcers, I think we can make the rest of the plan work."

I listen to the way she talks and take a good look at her; short gray hair under the subdued helmet and body armor, the drab gray jacket with black braid and tarnished buttons instead of the usual brightly colored Halloween Costume Steam Stripper outfit. "You've done this for real, haven't you?"

"Yep, today ain't my first day. Twenty-seven years with the FCG Foreign Legion; the last ten with the Humandroid Armored Infantry. Been to all the US of Federal Corporate A's downrange shit-holes at one time or another."

"Thank-you for your service, chief."

209

"Okay Goldie – couple of things. It's Sergeant Major, not chief, and do not *ever* call me *sarge* – it's *Sergeant Major* or *Sarn't*, understood?"

"I understand, Sergeant Major."

"Outstanding. Now, you want to thank me for my service? Take care of my Steam Enforcer problem and we'll call it all good."

"Yes Ma'am. We're on it."

"Geez," Frances says to Dolly. "That's the politest I've ever heard him be, and the longest he's ever gone without being a smartass."

Dolly stifles a laugh.

# Chapter Sixteen

The ruins of Morlock spread out beneath me. The four Steam Enforcers kick their way into the city like beach bullies at the geek's sand castle building extravaganza. Three massive land ironclads, the size and shape of the CSS Virginia on tremendous treads churn their own trail of destruction as they maneuver to intercept the Mecha-Godzilla quads. Each unleashes a rippling broadside as they cross in front of their formation; the leading Steam Enforcer bears the brunt of their fire, but their shells explode against it with no effect.

The Boilerplate infantry is massed behind them like Pickett's men on the third day, and they don't get off as lightly – falling shells tear gaping holes in their ranks, and many log out rather than face the incoming hate.

The land ironclads turn to withdraw, still firing their aft guns, concentrating on the infantry. In a surprising burst of speed, a Steam Enforcer sprints ahead and smashes a fist into the trailing land ironclad, then kicks it onto its side as its treads spin wildly seeking traction, seeking to escape. In an immense eruption of smoke and fire and steam, the stricken vehicle explodes as the Steam Enforcer stomps on it.

"Frances! That one, while he's separated from the pack!" I shout. The Steam Enforcers have colossal, eight-barrel Gatling guns instead of arms, and this one swings its guns up to target us as we zoom in to engage. Both our Freeze-O-Hacks are putting out tremendous plumes of ultra-cold, and we circle round and round it in opposite directions to deny it a clear shot.

Its feet stay planted and it spins at the waist through three hundred and sixty degrees to follow Frances; it fills the sky with torrents of anti-Frances fire, but as it gets colder, it moves slower and F. E. easily avoids all the flying unpleasantness. It freezes solidly immobile, and still we pour on the cold. The wreckage of the land ironclad at its feet is covered in frost flowers, and the moisture in the air around the Steam Enforcer condenses out as snow and coats the ground in an expanding circle.

"Gramogun!" Frances shouts as she swoops up to me. We hover close to it, careful to keep it between us and its unfrozen buddies. I access inventory item 558; the long brass Victrola horn of the Gramogun mounts itself to my shoulder. Frances has hers up as well, does a finger count *three-two-one-GO* and we blast away at it.

Or not, apparently. Nothing happens.

The horn on my shoulder vibrates some, but it doesn't seem to be putting out any noise. However, the Boilerplate infantry that had moved up when it stomped the land ironclad suddenly cover their ears, scream, and run away. The lenses on all of their stupid steampunk goggles have shattered, and with a sudden, gentle, noiseless *poof*, the frozen Steam Enforcer shivers into powder and collapses.

The three juggernauts are not particularly pleased at their compadre's treatment, and hurl staggering volumes of fire up after us. We dodge and twist and flit away, gain altitude, and suddenly there's fire coming at us from in front. Two fragile, ridiculous biplanes are hosing streams of lead at us. One flies into the Steam Enforcers' outgoing and explodes like a puffball; Dolly lands on the other, and with her glittering mantis appendages rends it to lint and sawdust.

Irish Shorty twists in the air in front of me, heading straight for the leading Enforcer. A gaudily painted triplane quarters in on him from the rear, fires on him, and wheels away even as it gets several hits on Shorty's jetpack, which sputs, fizzles, gouts steam and quits flying.

"Shorty ya wee bastard!" Scotty stoops after him, his leather kilt slapping in his slipstream. He nabs him like a kestrel on a field mouse, zoom-climbs above the triplane, and drops Shorty right into the cockpit. Shorty lands on the pilot's shoulders, and in a superb demonstration of Road Runner Physics, takes his place at the controls when he knocks the pilot through the bottom of the fuselage. The pilot flaps his arms, fails to fly on his own, logs out.

Shorty executes a snap roll and fires on friend and foe alike; everybody scatters, an Air Enforcer flies into a pusher biplane which crumples around him and falls from the sky. The sky is suddenly filled with dodging, ducking, twisting fliers most anxious to be somewhere Shorty *isn't*, except for a woman wearing traditional hunting pinks, white breeches and a cap with the ribbons down, who is mounted sidesaddle on a genuine twig besom. She flies up to Shorty, shoots a stream of goldy-purple sparkles at him from a star-tipped wand, and dives away cackling like a mad thing when he transmogrifies into a five-foot three inch anthropomorphic toad.

Toadish Shorty loops around and goes after the Flying Fox Huntress, and fires short bursts at her as he chases her lower and lower. She tosses vile yellow flying caltrops back at him which explode as they get close. He continues to pepper her with machine gun fire and finally gets her good; she's suddenly falling and spinning rather than flying. She hits the ground and disappears in a sparkly purplish explosion. Toadish shorty remains toadish, despite the alchemist's demise.

The three Steam Enforcers move at a slow walking pace, and smash through the center of Morlock; no subtlety or finesse – just crush the defenders and flatten a path straight through. They unleash a deluge of Gatling gun fire on anything that fires at them, and they pulverize every bunker and strongpoint they encounter. Both sides are putting all kinds of nasty flying stuff in the air, and we've all caught bits and pieces; the steam pack barely keeps my life bar topped up.

Burly, Pip, and Quiet Man loop off to the left of the oncoming behemoths; Aiden, Bucket Hat, and Scotty go right as Toadish Shorty dogfights with … well, everybody. Neon blue lightning bolts streak up from a clock tower on the right and zap right through Bucket hat. Just like in the cartoons, he's brilliantly illuminated from within, his skeleton is briefly visible, and then he dissipates in a falling cloud of dust. His hat spins to the ground.

Toadish Shorty executes a turn that almost pulls the wings off his triplane and dives directly into the lightning, firing as he goes. He never pulls out and never tries to; he smacks into the clock tower like a wood and canvas thunderbolt, accelerating all the way in. Great gouts of green and blue fire erupt from the tower as it explodes outward and collapses.

Burly, Pip, and Quiet Man get in behind the Steam Enforcers and let go with their Almost Universal Solvent throwers, aiming to saturate the extra super huge steam packs and power them down. Aiden and Scotty tangle with the Air Enforcers that provide air cover for their unstoppable colossi. The Air Enforcers attempt to swarm them, which only provides Aiden with more targets.

Supersonic fireflies whistle past my ears; someone's on my tail with unfriendly intent.

Rocket: Frances! Get the guy that's on Quantum!

Frances' steam-powered rocket cuts through the air and swats the plane from the sky. I dive on the mechanical monstrosity on my right; the wind forces tears from my eyes, and I seriously consider actually *using* my steampunk goggles.

"Thanks!" I yell over my shoulder. "I'm going in!"

The huge Enforcer smashes through another building, fires at the fleeing defenders, and then pivots at the waist to bring both Gatling guns to bear on me, even as it continues its unstoppable way forward. My Freeze-O-Hack is on deck again, and the blue stream of ultra-cold envelops it.

"Now!"

Frances and I activate our Gramoguns, and the Steam Enforcer silently erupts into soft, powdery ice crystals which gently settle on the troops fighting below – damn if it doesn't look like a big-ass Christmahanukwanzivus snow globe!

The remaining two behemoths grind through the city like metallic glaciers on legs, pulverizing buildings and human fighters below. I tuck in my arms and point my toes for better streamlining, increase my speed and aim for the nearest one.

An Air Enforcer collides with me hard enough to disorient me and partially deplete my life bar. He hangs on; even as we spin out of control he tries to shoot me in the face with an oversized hand cannon.

Wickedly serrated mantis appendages catch us, slow our spin, pull him off me and shred him like pulled pork. They snag another nearby Air Enforcer and rip him in half; he gouts steam and disappears – logged out.

"Are you okay?"

I look left and there's Dolly directly next to me, her eyes shining orange as she smiles.

"Okay ... okay ... " I tell her. "You're a *badass*."

"That's all I wanted to hear," she says, and zips away.

As much as I'd like to enjoy the vision that is Dolly in motion as she heads off to break things and hurt people, I've got company at two o'clock and they're closing fast.

"Ya bloody shitehawks!" Burly roars as he whooshes in to intercept. The Big, Bad, Battling Brit grabs an Air Enforcer in either hand and smashes them together like he's a kid making his Generic Joe corporate action figures fight. Pieces fly off of them; steam vents from every orifice. Burly's left with a double handful of nothing when they both log out. He shakes his fist and bellows, "Wankers! Quitters! Cheese-eating surrender monkeys!"

Yellow fireworks explode all around us.

"Down! Down!" Burly shouts.

~*~

I see a six pack of Hogwarts wannabes on the flat roof of a turreted tower. Five of them are in hooded black robes decorated with silver stars and moons and other cabalistic graffiti, and one is seated at each of the five points of a glowing star pentagon. Big number six stands tall in the center of the group, all decked out in a *Gandalf the White*

216

outfit, complete with pointy hat and staff. Mr. Wizard wields the staff like a rocket launcher, and fiery yellow spheres of thaumaturgical nastiness shoot from the end and whiz up at us. I turn and fall towards them with the terminal velocity of de-orbiting space junk.

*Let me! Let me!*

The hack ax forms and morphs to hack gun without my calling it from inventory, points itself and fires a tremendous blue-white sphere of incandescence. The top third of the tower vanishes in a blinding flare; what's left of it has run and melted like a candle in the August Texas sunshine.

Voices in my head is usually not a good thing, but every time *this* little voice pipes up, my mutant hack ax does something unexpected … and becomes orders of magnitude more effective …

The Steam Enforcer spins up its Gatling guns and burns through ammo like it'll be fined for every cartridge it doesn't expend. It tracks me and puts up a blizzard of fist-sized pellets; expended shotgun shells the size of kindergarteners pile up around its feet. Frances is on the edge of the cloud and flits through with the agility of a double-jointed hummingbird. No such luck for the kid; what's coming at me is so dense that an anorexic mosquito couldn't get through.

This is going to *hurt!*

Real men don't log out.

Dolly pixilates in front of me in a flash. Wings balloon from her back, shielding me from the Wall O' Lead. I speed forward and we lock arms, amidst the explosions below us, the enemy Air Enforcers swirling all around us, the huge mechanized monster spraying us with its Gatling shotgun.

"You're wonderful, Doll," I tell her as we kiss, "my everything."

"Your everything?" she asks as more pellets hammer into her metallic wings.

"My everything. We need some time alone, a long time alone … "

"After the battle, Quantum," she says.

"After the battle."

I jet into the air, up and over her wings and arrow down into the dead space where the Steam Enforcer's guns won't bear. It spins and twists and tries to swat me with its Gatling gun arms. As I dodge, my Freeze-O-Hack comes up. I hover over its shoulder and give it the mother of all brain freezes.

Frances waves at me from her vantage point over its other shoulder and points to her Gramogun.

She finger counts three-two-one and we activate our banshee horns. The giant, frozen, metallic head silently *Chicxulubs* into a bazillion icy pixels; the monstrous decapitated body locks up in mid step, wobbles and falls with a thunderous impact, like King Kong landing on West 33rd Street.

I hover in place and spend just that little bit too long admiring my handiwork. Another Air Enforcer attempts an intercept and swipes at me with a boarding cutlass as she swoops past. She makes a short banking turn and comes back for a second pass.

*Let me handle this.*

"Who said that?" I shout as my hack ax grows spikes and blades and hooks, and seemingly of its own volition eviscerates her as she dives at me. The screaming, steaming, mortally wounded Air Enforcer spirals away and disappears as she logs out.

One Steam Enforcer left.

~*~

Aiden and Dolly flank me now. Frances is behind us; the remaining UK Assassins form up on the four of us.

"Bloody 'ell, mate!" Burly cries as he zips past me. He takes out a Boilerplate Air Enforcer with a throwing star the size of a turkey platter. "Number nineteen, boys!" he shouts over his shoulder to the battling Brits whooshing in the air behind him.

The final Steam Enforcer fires its enormous Gatling shotguns at us, the barrels blur around a central axis with one mission, and one mission only – complete annihilation. Our group parts down the middle and we zip wide to avoid the pellets. Aiden beelines towards the Steam Enforcer, firing his Slice Bang.

I'm in front of the big metal bastard seconds later, and hose its Gatling guns with my AUS sprayer – best to deal with them first.

An Air Enforcer rockets directly at me, ko-wakazashi in one hand and trench hawk in the other. He is so focused on me that he never sees Scotty blindside him from behind. Scotty hovers, laugh, forks two fingers at Burly and darts away to seek another target.

The Gatling guns soften into uselessness and the clunker swats at me like I'm a particularly annoying stinging insect. While its attention is focused on me, Frances Euphoria scissors in behind the Steam Enforcer at top speed. She cuts loose on it with her Freeze-O-Hack and doesn't let up until it's ceased all motion and frozen solid. Again with the Gramogun treatment, and Frosty the Five Story Snowman collapses into a whopping great heap of fluffy powdered retro robot ice crystals.

"We did it!"

I do a twist in the air and regroup with Dolly.

"We did it!" I shout.

Frances smacks into me a few moments later, latching onto me.

"We won!" She hugs me tightly, uses her jet pack to twirl me in the air. I look over her red hair to catch Dolly watching us.

Aiden zips by and fires on one of the remaining Air Enforcers, who apparently decides that he who fights and runs away, lives. He's trailed by Burly, who pumps his fist in celebration and Pip, who sprays his Hose Gun like it's a bottle of cheap champagne. From our vantage point above Morlock, I can see the battle has changed beneath us. There are fires and clouds of smoke, but what's most important is that we've smashed their giant game-changers and crushed the Boilerplate Army's morale – the NPCs are surrendering and the human players are logging out.

"What now?" I ask.

Lightning cracks above us. A portal appears in the sky, rimmed in yellow. It pulsates, grows in size until it's thirty yards in diameter.

"We got company!" I say, aiming my hack at the portal.

Reapers spill out, riding steam-powered motorcycles, followed by Reapers in jetpacks. A figure in a blue orb of actinic fire floats out of the center of the portal.

"It's him … " Frances says. "It's him!"

# Chapter Seventeen

Strata Godsick.

My mutant hack comes up and I zap the blue orb with everything I got. My blast hits the orb and dissipates; a squirt gun would have had more effect. Frances takes a shot – still nothing.

"What do we do, Rocket!?"

I back away; the steam from my jetpack billows out in front of me.

Rocket: His stats are off the charts! Look at his life bar, his advanced abilities bar!

"Glad to see you're a fan," I yell, "but what do we do?"

The blue orb fades. Godsick's Reaper mask resembles a deer's skull, elongated to cover his face and topped with massive antlers. He's in black back-and-breastplate armor with a large blue jewel mounted over his heart. A black cowl and cloak fastened to the shoulders of the armor hangs past his floating feet.

Electricity zigzags between Godsick's antlers forming a lightning ball at the apex of his headgear. It smashes into me before I can move and hurls me into the city below.

Rocket: Holy crap!

I smash through the bell tower of a cathedral, through the leaded roof, through a wall, another wall and through a ceiling into a classroom. My life bar drops to 25%. I would have been dead at least twice if Ray Steampunk hadn't boosted my life bar to 250%.

I'm cradled in a nest of debris, which is lumpy and uncomfortable. My *everything* hurts, my eyes won't focus, my pocket watch broke, and I think I may have peed in my garish steampunk costume.

"Geez! Did anybody get the transponder code of the aeros that hit me?" I ask, and I track my trajectory into *Our Lady of Great Agony* cathedral through the series of perfectly aligned Quantum-shaped holes. I idly wonder how they managed to get the stars, planets, and tweety birds inside to circle around my head like that. I move to shake it off and get back in the game.

With a thunderous, dubbed-in, special effects roar, a Reaper astride a steam-powered motorcycle crashes through the classroom door to make his obligatory dramatic and über-masculine entrance. He backflips off the bike and it smashes through into the next classroom and explodes. All he needs is a spray can of *Rutting Buck* air freshener and the *Arlington AT&T Cowboys Cheerleaders* in a kick line behind him to complete the effect.

I sigh at the predictable lameness of it all.

"Quantum Hughes," he rumbles, as he cracks his knuckles and takes a menacing step towards me. He's all leather and muscles and spikes and horns and sharp things, and veins crawl and swell on the side of his bull neck.

I am so *not* in the mood for this no-neck mofo.

I shoot him down with my wrist gun and step over him, not even stopping to crush his skull mask with my stomper. Sometimes, the pleasures in life must be postponed.

223

Rocket: Equip the binoculars I gave you. There's a bunch of added features and scanners that aren't *exactly* world appropriate, but should help. Look for a power source, a discontinuity, anything …

My hand comes up and I find item 557.

The rubber eyecups mold to my eye sockets, and the tableau in the sky magnifies 5X, 10X, 20X, 40X, the images razor sharp and gyro stabilized. Dolly hovers between Strata Godsick and Frances Euphoria now. Her appendages have multiplied, the sharpened points bending over her body like multiple scorpion's stingers.

Rocket: Never mind her! Focus on Strata – look for the red indicator.

The image jumps to 80X, 160X. My former partner's eye coverings are red; black makeup occludes his facial features. A green line moves left and right as it scans his body. It stops over the jewel on his chest and a blinking red reticle appears.

"The jewel," I say aloud. "I think I found his weakness."

~*~

I'm in the air seconds later. The Steam Pack has boosted my life bar to 30%, but if Strata does the *Flaming Antler Blast* on me again, then stick me with a fork cuz I am *done*! There's only one solution: I've got to get to the jewel on his chest.

My mutant hack morphs into a large blade as I begin my ascent.

*I'm ready.*

The voice comes to me and I glance left and right. An enormous explosion overhead; the shock wave buffets me and I see double-ended mushroom cloud of steam.

"Dolly!" I shout, as soon as I realize what Godsick has done. Advanced abilities activated, I appear next to Frances moments later. In front of both of us is a slowly dissipating cloud of steam.

"Let me handle this, Frances," I say, moving in front of her.

"I've got your back," Aiden says, on the other side of Frances now.

"Is Dolly ... ?"

I can't even form the words.

"No, she's not," he says, "she'll respawn in The Loop."

"Strata!" I scream at the glowing red eyes behind the wall of steam. "Face me!"

The silence is deafening. The action around us, the explosions below us, the lightning cracking in the sky behind Strata Godsick – none of it matters to me now as I stare into the eyes of my enemy, a man who tried to have me killed, a man responsible for the deaths of hundreds of people. *My former partner.*

"You coward!" I scream. "You shitbird! Killing people in virtual worlds!? What kind of sick ... "

His hand comes up.

"Quantum!" I turn to find a blue orb forming around Frances Euphoria. She screams as sparks of electricity jolt through her body.

Rocket: He's preventing her from logging out!

"DAMN YOU, STRATA!"

I race forward with my blade at my side and I'm instantly repelled. The force sends me reeling backwards, straight into Morning Assassin.

"Frances!" I cry as my mutant hack shrinks. I reach my fingers to the blue orb around her body. The shock slams through me, blasts me away, tosses me backwards. My vision red tinges, the steam pack chugs to keep me alive, and I can't access my inventory.

"Log her out, Rocket!"

Rocket: I can't! It's feeding back through her NV Visor; the SpiderDoc is limiting the damage, but he's gaining on it. He's keeping her just alive enough in there to really kill her up here!

"Aiden! Aiden!" I turn to find Morning Assassin staring at Godsick with true fear in his eyes. "What do we do!?"

Aiden has no words.

A golden orb appears in front of us and a being of light steps out. I recognized the slicked back hair immediately.

~*~

A golden flame ignites in Ray Steampunk's hand. The flame leaps into the air, falls onto the blue orb of death that's frying the life from Frances Euphoria, and bursts it like a soap bubble. I swoop down to catch Frances.

"Are you okay?" I ask, slapping her cheek. "Frances! Speak to me, dammit!"

She lifts her hand and a logout button materializes. One press of the button and her body pixilates.

"Strata Godsick," Ray Steampunk says, the gold indicator shining over his head. "We meet again."

Godsick smiles and waits.

Using his assassin abilities, Aiden appears behind Godsick in a flash. He swings his Slice Bang at Godsick's neck and is stopped by a single raised finger. Aiden disappears again, and reappears in front of the head of the Reapers. He executes a flying kick. Godsick catches his foot between thumb and pointer finger, nonchalantly grabs his other ankle, and rips him in half.

Godsick's eyes flare and Morning Assassin explodes into a cloud of steam.

"You bastard!" I race forward, fists raised.

I smash into an invisible wall. I slam my fists against something insubstantial yet solid, preventing me from reaching Strata Godsick.

Ray Steampunk's voice echoes through my skull.

"You've done well for yourself, Strata, profiting from a glitch."

Godsick tries to blast the NPC with blue antler lightning. Steampunk lifts his finger and the electricity fizzles into nothing.

"All to find your son," Steampunk says. "You've taken countless lives, grown a company and destroyed your friendships. You've become a murderer and I … "

227

Another blast, this time orders of magnitude larger than the first. Ray Steampunk's body disintegrates. The pixels spray out, only to be sucked back into a vortex where Steampunk was just floating. They reform his body in a matter of seconds.

"And I helped you ... "

Rocket: Quantum! EMS is on the way! Frances is ...

"She's what!?" I cry, watching the exchange. I slam my fist against the invisible wall. I back up and jet into it, shoulder first; it bounces me off like a big invisible trampoline.

Rocket: Log out, Q, log out!

Ray Steampunk points at Strata. "I know where your son, Luther, is trapped." His finger comes up and another golden flame appears. "And now, so does Quantum Hughes."

The golden flame appears in front of my face. As soon as I touch it, the flame is transferred to my inventory list, item 568.

Strata Godsick's body folds into a thin line, like the electrons draining out of a cathode ray tube-tech TV when the power's cut. He appears directly in front of me, on the other side of the invisible wall. He brings his fist back and hammers it into the barrier; a crack appears in front of my face.

Rocket: Log out! Log out!

"No," I say as I glare Strata Godsick down. "Bring it on you piece of shit!"

I can see Ray Steampunk over Godsick's shoulder, one finger raised and his black eyes wide open. A logout point appears in front of me.

228

"No!" I scream as my hand is forced up to the logout point. "No, Ray! No! PUT MY HAND DOWN, RAY!"

Strata Godsick hits the invisible wall again. The crack spreads.

My finger comes down on the logout button.

~*~

"Log me back in!" I cry, as soon as I've spit out the oxygen mouthpiece. "Log me in! Goddammit Rocket, LET ME LOG BACK IN!"

"Relax, man," an unfamiliar voice says.

Rocket says, "Quantum, Frances is out of the vat and the ambulance is on the way. I've asked Zedic to help! Hold tight for a minute and we'll get you out!"

I kick my legs against the silicone. "I don't ... I DON'T WANT OUT!"

"Chill man," Zedic says.

"Who the hell are you?" I feel a hand touch my arm and I shake it off as best as I can.

"Dream Team, just like you," he says, "Quit squirming, I'll get you out."

As soon as my arm is free I tear off the NV Visor. I'm sitting up now, looking around the room even though the lights are still too damn bright. "Dammit! Rocket! Let me log back in! I had him ... he was right there! RIGHT THERE!"

229

Rocket says, "You *didn't* have him; he had you – he was gonna do you next! Frances is injured, Quantum! *Real World Injured!* We have to deal with this first."

"Dammit!" I slam my fist into the silicone gel. My vision blurs into focus and I see the ArachnaMed SpiderDoc dangling from the ceiling, administering oxygen to Frances and monitoring her vitals.

"What happened in there?" Zedic is behind me now, placing the NV Visor in its docking station.

"Strata Godsick! Rocket! Strata Godsick did this!"

"I know! I was watching!" Rocket's voice softens. "Frances, the gurney is going to lift on its own now … "

"Frances! Are you okay?" I ask as I push myself out of the vat. I slip and hit the ground hard, ignoring the pain. "Is she okay!?"

A muscular arm comes under me and helps me up. "Relax, man," Zedic says, "you need to take it easy."

"Take it easy!? WE HAD HIM! I … I HAD HIM!"

"EMS is here, Frances," Rocket says. "We'll get you to the hospital."

Two emergency aid Humandroids enter the room. One of them speaks to Rocket for a moment as I try to catch my breath.

"Help me up, dammit. I'm going with Frances!"

"You're in no condition … " Zedic starts to say.

"Don't you tell me about my condition – *I'm going with Frances!"*

230

## Chapter Eighteen

Seeing Frances Euphoria in the hospital bed only reminds me of how real all this is, whether or not it takes place in a dreamworld, or right here in Baltimore. It's funny how quickly I forget that. Her once red lips are slightly blue, her skin a shade paler than normal – everything comes down on me all at once and increases my despair and confusion. What is real? What isn't real? What does it matter when someone you care for has been injured? Digital or otherwise, the future – my future – is both.

"Are you ready?" Rocket asks. He clears his throat. "Quantum."

"Sorry … "

The gangly man-child is standing next to a portable haptic chair across from Frances' hospital bed. He has an NV Visor on his head with the optical interface flipped up. He looks as anxious as I feel. I don't want to, and I know it will be quick, but I need to log back into the Proxima Galaxy to transfer the flame Ray Steampunk gave me to Rocket's inventory list so he can examine it.

One more glance at Frances.

The doctor said that she'll recover in a week or so, but seeing her strapped into the hospital bed with tubes stuck in everywhere, a blood pressure cuff around her leg, a breathing device jammed in her nostrils, a heart monitor displaying wave forms and her wrists restrained makes my heart twist into a bitter knot. What I wouldn't give to unleash my fists on Godsick's face, to do to him exactly what he has done to Frances Euphoria and to so many others. To become the Reaper.

"Let's make this quick," I tell Rocket.

"Very quick," he says sitting next to me. "You log in, I log in, you transfer the flame to me and we log out. Simple."

"The Loop?"

"If that's where you want to go."

"And you sure you don't want a haptic chair?"

He shakes his head. "I only plan to be in for a moment. Once I get Ray's flame, I can examine it back at the office."

"Got it."

Pulling the visor over my eyes, I relax into the chair and hear the Brian Eno tone. The wavelengths come a few moments later, picking up their speed. A spawn point appears and I select The Loop, specifically, my hotel room.

Digital nature takes its course. Feedback showers, acid brain. My hotel room at the Mondegreen blurs into focus and a sense of contentment overcomes me.

I'm sitting on the bed in the flophouse, watching rain splash against the window. Thunder rumbles, lightning does its thing. *Home – a much needed kick in the ass.*

I don't need to look over my shoulder to know that there's a sinking sailboat pegged to the wall. My Luckies are on the dresser; my mirror is next to the window. I'm more familiar with this room than I am my own body in the real world.

A blip of light appears and Rocket steps out. He's dressed more or less the same as he dresses in the real world, but he's much buffer in his avatar body. Not quite Rollins, but not far off.

"Hit the digi-gym lately?" I ask.

"From time to time," he says, flexing his biceps and assuming the classic *which way to the beach* pose.

"Easy, cowboy."

My inventory list appears in front of me and I retrieve item 568, Ray Steampunk's golden flame. It floats in the air between Rocket and me.

"Interesting," he says. "I'll need to analyze it … it's definitely not a weapon though."

"It is a numerical code." I turn to find Dolly on the bed behind me. She's in her red dress and diamond necklace, one leg crossed over the other with her back against the wall. A hotbody at ease.

"Hey, Doll."

"Hiya."

"A spawn point?" Rocket asks her.

"Yes, the coordinates to a Proxima World. Let me see it."

The golden flame floats over to Dolly, illuminating her porcelain skin.

"What did Ray Steampunk tell you about it?" she asks me.

"He said that it was the location of Strata Godsick's son."

"So he's stuck in a Proxima World?" Dolly asks, her finger dancing along the tip of the flame.

"Apparently."

"That's interesting … "

"I've been too distracted to think about it," I admit.

Rocket asks, "Can you decipher it, Doll?"

"Dolly," I tell him flatly.

"Dolly."

"Not much to decipher; However, they have been scrambled … I'll need to play around with the numbers for a moment … "

Numbers appears in the air, scrolling up and down. Dolly watches the numbers move by without blinking. The numbers spiral together like a small tornado, a few numbers separating from the digital storm and floating over to Rocket.

"That's the last one," Dolly says as the tenth number stops in front of him. "Take a screenshot. These are the coordinates to a Proxima World known as Tritania."

"Tritania?" I ask. "What type of world is it?"

"A fantasy world," she says, "with three floating continents."

"Got it. I'll begin preliminary research." Rocket raises his hand to log out. "Are you coming?"

I look to the beautiful gal lying on my bed in her skin-tight red dress. My real world problems come to me and I gulp them down. When in doubt, escape.

"I think I'll stay for a while … things are, *easier* in here sometimes."

"I understand." Rocket presses the logout button. "See you on the other side, Q."

**The End**

## High Fantasy: The Feedback Loop Book Three

The action-packed third book in the Feedback Loop Series is out now!

Quantum Hughes and the Dream Team dive to Tritania, an MMORPG fantasy Proxima World filled with dragons, orcs, floating continents, and magic. With the clock ticking, and his problems in the real world growing, including his legal troubles and his blossoming relationship with Frances Euphoria, Quantum is forced to make a decision that could change his life forever.

The stakes are higher than they've ever been.

Steam, The Loop, Tritania and the real world – four worlds collide in the third installment of The Feedback Loop Series. **The thin line between dream and reality is pixilated.**

Note: There's a sample of Chapter one at the back of the book.

# Back of the Book Shit

**Dear Reader,**

The research for this book was mostly done through visual mediums, most notably the movies *Steamboy* and *Sucker Punch*. I wanted the world of Steam to be multi-faceted and feel authentic, even though it seems trivial to Quantum. In the book, we visit Locus and Morlock, but there are other cities to explore and dungeons to conquer on Steam.

When I first set out to write this book, I figured it would be a one-off affair. Quantum and Frances go to Steam, they get the information they want, and they return to the real world. Boom – novel finished. As it turns out, Steam is too big of a world to appear in just one book and Ray Steampunk is a character with vast stores of information. So expect more steamy shenanigans (that doesn't mean sex) in the future.

The next book in the Feedback Loop series will be called High Fantasy. It will be available at the end of November, beginning of December. I'm looking forward to this book, as it will add an even bigger fantasy element to the series. Expect some dragons, orcs, giants and all things Tolkien (or Martin?) in the next installment.

Plus, The Loop, Steam, the Battling Brits, Aiden, Dolly, posturing Reapers and more.

**Relation to my other series.**

The Feedback Loop series takes place twenty-five years before my other sci-fi series, Life is a Beautiful Thing. I plan to continue writing in this world indefinitely through these two series and more in the future. In Steampunk is Dead, we are introduced to

Humandroids, pollutes and iNet – all staples in Life is a Beautiful Thing – which takes place in 2083, a year I chose as it would be my 100th birthday if I live that long (please say I won't – I'd hate to see how wrong I am about the future).

Quantum's struggle with his own humanity is also something that has come to the forefront in this series. Like most of us, he's full of contradictions and opinions. The fact that he won't take a cybernetic upgrade is an example of this. In a Proxima World, he would happily take a replacement part, but not in the real world. I find this to be the most humanizing thing about this character. I can't tell you how many times I've said or done something knowing that it goes against my convictions or the pre-conceived notion of my convictions.

**Words and more words.**

If you've read my other series, Life is a Beautiful Thing, you've like noticed my obsession with word play and unique words. We share a language that increases in vastness daily. The Feedback Loop series borrows from old words, hard-boiled detective sayings and phrases, as well as language that has fallen out of popularity. Finding these words is part of my research process. I'd like to personally thank the Internet and the people in charge of listicles for making Q's dialogue possible. (What is a listicle? An article + a list. Aka clickbait).

Thank you, Internet Jesus. I'll sacrifice something later.

**Thanks and more thanks.**

Much appreciation goes out to Kay who beta read this piece. The best... the best! Ben made some steamy suggestions that helped with my research. Keep lotioning, I want some socks. Others provided encouragement through their reviews and emails. You know who you are. To my editor, George C. Hopkins, your dedication to this series and suggestions on this book in particular have made Steampunk is Dead truly something to be remembered. If you found a very familiar quote in the book, or a reference that seemed too good to be true, it was likely George's suggestion. Trust your editor, folks!

Yours in sanity,

Harmon Cooper

Writer.harmoncooper@gmail.com

**High Fantasy**

The Feedback Loop Book Three

<u>SAMPLE</u>

Harmon Cooper

Edited by George C. Hopkins

# Chapter One

Aiden is in a basketball jersey with the initials M.A. across his back. In his left hand is his WalMacy's net shopping bag full of cactus and across his chest are ten horseshoes held to his body by a leather belt. A fly swatter is tucked into the front of his basketball shorts alongside a pair of rusty gardening shears.

"Do you see Tony?" he asks me, roller-skating in a circle. He wears a pair of vintage roller skates with leather uppers and hardened toes.

Cold BBs of rain soak our clothes and pockets of lightning add shadow to our faces. On my knees, I again glance down through the rooftop skylight at the card game below. My Reaper skull, item 551, allows me to see the gridlines that make up The Loop. I can also see NPCs, although their names aren't displayed.

"What's he look like again?"

"Fat, lots of hair, big sunglasses, little mustache."

Tony Clifton was a new crime boss who had partnered up with Chinatown's Scarface Charlie. Pushing Riotous through greasy food joints and massage parlors was his MO, concreting people's feet was his favorite pastime. He wasn't as bad as Charlie, not the type to use a head crusher on a first date, but if there's anything I've learned in The Loop it is this: the good get bad and the bad get worse.

"Here comes the Godfather now."

"How many, Quantum?"

"Eight, including the big cheese."

My ocular feed shows a man with a distended belly entering the room. His greased up cowlick and the outline of his sunglasses confirms it – this is our man. My skull mask dematerializes as it returns to my inventory list. I place my boxing glove on my hand, item 32, and twist the handle on my antique selfie stick, item 99. I've been whipped to death by a selfie stick before – it hurts like the dickens. Item 353, my football pads, add some bulk to my frame as does my vintage Bengals football helmet, item 271. Just in case I need to slice and dice, item 40, my serrated elephant tusk, hangs from a loop on my belt.

"That reminds me ... " My inventory list comes up and I scroll to item 273 – cleats with metal spikes. They appear on my feet, lace themselves up.

"Remember," I tell Aiden, "no conventional weapons. If you die, do not respawn. That's the only rule."

"Got it," he says with a wolfish grin.

~*~

Our "Nonconventional Weapons Rule" means that we can't blow through the ceiling as we normally would. Luckily, Aiden has already worked his way around this self-imposed restriction.

"Just leap over holding onto this," he tells me as he fastens the rope to a rooftop air conditioner unit. "Activate your advanced abilities and rocket through the window. I'll hit the other side at the same time. Nothing to it."

"Don't kill Tony," I remind him.

"Same to you."

I jam my selfie stick in my belt, keeping my boxing glove on my right hand. I'm on the edge of the rooftop seconds later, holding the rope with one hand and waiting for Aiden's signal. The cold rain picks up and runs into my eyes.

"Come on, Dolly, lighten up, will ya?" I ask the sky.

The rain stops completely, but the clouds stay dark.

"Thanks, Doll."

Aiden's finger comes up and he twists it in the air like a mini lasso. Pushing off the ledge, I shoot out over the rooftop and I activate my advanced abilities bar, giving me both the juice and the ability to violate the Einsteinian space-time continuum. Cleats plus glass equals Shattersville. I land in the room and roll out, brandishing my selfie stick.

One of the button men watching the card game goes for his gat, but I reenact the Caning of Senator Charles Sumner and he drops like two hundred pounds of bad habit in a cheap suit. I give his face the cube steak treatment as I dance a Flamenco a la Cleats with my selfie stick clenched between my teeth – *Olé*!

A ferret-faced, greasy little weasel of a man is somewhat faster than his card playing buddies, and even in slo-mo gets his .45 out and pointed right at my heart, just as Aiden frisbees a horseshoe into the back of his head. *Holy horseshoe headache, Batman!* Mr. Mustelidae's cigarette, chewing gum and toothpick fly out of his mouth as he hits the table and scatters the chips, but he maintains a death grip on his cards, and no wonder – he's holding a royal flush.

I'm sorry to see a good hand wasted like that, but I've got more important things to deal with at the moment. I give the next goomba a little Joe Frasier and think about throwing in a little Tyson-Holyfield II action when I'm whacked from behind with a crowbar. Stars, planets and tweety-birds circle my head; my ears ring, my nose runs and I release a cloud of flatus as the ghost of Neil deGrasse Tyson laughs and points. My life bar drops by 25% and I can't make my hands or feet obey my commands as I reel forward from the blow.

Aiden to the rescue with a pair of flying horseshoes, which catch the crowbar swinging no-goodnik right in the cakehole, and lodge there like a pair of politically incorrect cartoon Ubangi Lip Plates. He keels over backwards, and I shake off the effects of his rolled steel love-tap. I drop my AA bar for a moment to sink a hard right into the beezer of the chubby-cheeked shylock just getting a grip on his gun. He squeezes the trigger in response and fires the round out the side of his jacket and into Tony Clifton's foot, who screams like the lunch whistle at the Big Sissy Manufacturing Company.

My finger comes up and a pot of lawsuit-temperature McStarbucks Ultra-Caff CappEspresso, item 9, materializes in my other hand. A flick of my wrist and the overpriced hipster tipple parboils another black-suited palooka's wedding tackle. Like a wheeled Tonya Harding-Gillooly, Aiden launches into a Triple Axel and snaps his shopping bag o' cactus straight into the man's already uncomfortable nether region. The brawny bruiser falls to his knees, face plants, and twitches spasmodically.

Advanced abilities redux. I charge forward and put my football-helmeted head right in the breadbasket of the zoot-suited triggerman nearest the door. He folds in the middle and his spine snaps like a breadstick as I knock him right out of his pointy-toed sharkskin shoes and neat little porkpie hat. I can almost see the ref throw the yellow flag like they used to when football still had rules.

Bullets break the sound barrier above me; I drop my selfie stick and get a firm grip on my serrated elephant tusk. I'm just about to engage in some antique ivory sliceage and diceage when somebody's copper-jacketed hate mail connects with my shoulder, spins me around and knocks my life bar down another 10%.

I turn to see Aiden use his garden shears like a gladius on the triggerman who just ruined a perfectly good pair of vintage football shoulder pads. I take this moment to do a little sawing on the man's throat beneath me. Saw, saw, saw goes the saw and bleed, bleed, bleed goes the throat and I'm done before the nursery rhyme can finish.

"All right! All right! Ya got me!" Tony Clifton has his hands in the air now. Aiden is behind him, the tip of his fly swatter pressed into the Godfather's ear.

"It's a shiv?" I ask. The mobster beneath me coughs, causing the gaping wound on his neck to bleed out even more.

"Yeah," Aiden says, "I thought you knew."

"A shiv is a conventional weapon."

"Is it? You know, the serrated elephant tusk could also be considered a conventional weapon."

A caddish cugine near one of the smashed windows coughs. The man tries to stand, tumbles forward in a slump as his digital ghost exits his body.

Tony Clifton barks. "You two ain't gettin' away with this! This is Scarface Charlie's territory – I know people!"

246

"Looks like everyone you know is either dead or dying," I say as I approach the top banana. Tony tries to move; Aiden responds by pressing the sharpened end of the fly swatter deeper into the head honcho's earhole.

"What's the big idea, Mac? You tryin' ta poke my brain or somethin'?"

I use my elephant tusk to lift his chin so that Tony's looking right at me with his big brown eyes. "I'm only going to ask you this once – where's Dirty Dave?"

"That slimeball? You come here for scum like that!?"

"Tell him what he wants to know," Aiden says. "Otherwise you'll be taking a trip to the … What's the word for an ear doctor?"

"An Otolaryngologist," Tony says matter-of-factly. "I see mine regularly. You should too."

"I'll look into it."

"That's great," I tell both of them, "but we ain't here for a checkup. Where's Dirty Dave?"

"That cafone owes me money!" he growls. A vein appears on the side of his head.

"How much does he owe you?"

"More credit than you got!"

Aiden gets my drift and steps back, allowing me to sink a fist into the boss man's schnozzle. "Dirty Dave," I say as blood trickles out of his nose. "Tell us where he is or you'll … what do you mafia-types say? *Sleep with the fishes?* I'll give you a new pair of concrete DisNikes and toss you off The Pier. Tell us where he is and I won't kill you. How's that sound?"

He curls his lips, weighs his options.

"There are some real hungry fish at The Pier," I tell him, "piranhas too. You got options here, Tony."

"I'm the one that put those piranhas there," he admits, "and you're right, they are hungry. I don't know why you're so interested in that babbo."

"We have our reasons," I tell him.

"Dirty Dave is here in Chinatown, practically under your noses."

"No shit, Sherlock, but *where* in Chinatown?"

Aiden gives Gotti-light a quick rabbit punch with his free hand.

"What the hell was that for!?"

"Hurry up."

"Relax already," Tony says. "I'm talkin', ain't I?"

"Not fast enough," I tell the bloody kingpin.

"Chinese grocery. Up the street."

"You got him in the freezer?"

"Yeah," he tells me, "hanging from a meat hook like the carcass that he is."

"Good, thanks Tony," I say. "Do what you gotta do, Aiden."

"Can I borrow your elephant tusk?" he asks.

"Not a problem." I drop the tusk on the table and turn to the door.

"You said you wouldn't kill me!" Tony shouts, spittle spraying out of his mouth.

"I won't," I say over my shoulder. "He will."

~*~

Nothing like a digital smoke to celebrate a successful endeavor. We came, we saw, we conquered, and we did it without the aid of conventional weaponry. What can I say? I'm not one to brag but Morning Assassin and I are good, real good.

The door pops open and Aiden steps out sporting the *Passion of the Christ* look.

"He was a bleeder."

"Care for a drag?" I say as I ash my cigar, item 30, on the floor.

"The last time I tried one of your death sticks I nearly coughed up a lung."

"This is much more refined than your typical square. It's a Cuban of the best quality, the type of cigar Castro would have starved peasants for. Besides, you don't have lungs," I remind him. We laugh together, long and hard.

"Well then," I say as I press the end of my cigar into my palm. Sure, it affects my life bar a little, but it'll replenish itself. "Shall we see about Dirty Dave?"

Aiden takes the lead. As he walks, his bloodied basketball getup disappears and his black clothes return, in much the same way a mirage blurs into focus. My Bengals helmet dematerializes but I keep my pads on, as they are comfortable and I can't be bothered to change clothing.

We walk down a flight of stairs, and a single flickering light illuminates the small stairwell. I think of my problems in the real world – my body is currently in Frances Euphoria's hospital room, where it has been for the last… no sense in checking because I don't want to know. I'd rather just stay here in The Loop, the vice-ridden fleshpot where there are no consequences to my actions, no Federal Bureau of Investigation and Intelligence Gathering trying to pin something on me. Not gonna lie – I'm at home in a place where drugstore cowboys with chips on their shoulders call all the shots; where ritzy skirts turn tricks in back alleys for bumps of Riotous; where clip joints and can houses outnumber petting pantries ten to one; where the odds are always against you. The answer to *the Sprawl*, a place of techno-filth and digi-violence.

Almost-home.

"You know, Dolly lives around here," Aiden says as we exit the building.

"In Chinatown?" I ask. One glance up the street and I see red paper lanterns and banners with Asian characters crossing from one side to the other. "I thought … Well, I don't know what I thought, but her living situation never crossed my mind."

"Typical … " Aiden's eyes flash orange and then return to their normal color.

"What, we never talked about it!"

"She lives up there, in the apartment above a sushi joint." He points to a small room on the third story of a building about fifty paces away. The red curtains are drawn, lit from behind.

"I should stop by sometime."

"You should," Aiden says.

A rickshaw driver pedals by, nearly knocking me out of my pads. "Watch it, buddy!" I say.

"The rickshaw drivers in Chinatown follow their own rules," Aiden explains as he steps around a man selling fried fish on a stick.

One click of my inventory list later and my BFG 9000 – item 100 – is in my hands. A huge green ball of plasma explodes out of the weapon, vaporizing the rickshaw.

Aiden laughs. "Man! That is some weapon. Dirty Dave?"

"Yup. Big, right?"

"Big is an understatement," Aiden says, taking a step closer to me. "The dual proton high intensity pulser is one of a kind. The hard shell anti-matter containment box can take quite a bit of heat and the two handles on top – one Kevlar and one titanium – are shock resistant and allow for the weapon to be held in a variety of ways. Care if I take a shot?"

"By all means."

As soon as Aiden takes the BFG he aims it at the man selling fried fish. "What the big idea!" the man shouts. "You no shoot me! You want fish, you eat fish! Free! Please!"

"An L22 responsive trigger on a lightweight titanium alloy spring grip makes for maneuverability and quick firing." Aiden swivels right and up, shoots a green ball of plasma at a taxi above us. The taxi comes crashing down, taking out the corner of a tchotchke shop.

"You know, we should do this more often," I say.

"What? Come to Chinatown and shoot at things?"

"Bingo."

~*~

"Where's the freezer?" I ask a woman behind the counter at the Chinese supermarket. She's a classy chassis, Asian, with the right mix of lean and fierce. The green icon over her head indicates she's an NPC.

"No freezer," she tells me. "Buy something or leave."

Aiden appears behind her and presses my BFG into her back.

"Gotta love those assassin abilities," I say, taking a few steps closer to the checkout counter. "Care to tell us again about the freezer you don't have?"

The woman kicks her leg back, right into Aiden's digital family jewels; she flips over his body before he can fire a shot. Her feet hit the ground and she pushes off, flipping forward again and landing next to Aiden and using her momentum to strip him of his weapon.

The last thing I see is a giant green flash.

# About the Author

Originally from Austin, Texas, I kept Austin weird for a quarter of a century before moving to Asia. I've lived and traveled extensively through the Asian continent, staying in everything from Mongolian yurts to traditional Japanese homes on the outskirts of Kyoto. I've hitchhiked across the Punjab, met child goddesses in Nepal, visited the Tiger's Nest in Bhutan, encountered Green Tara near the Kazakhstan border, drunk soju with America's Finest in Korea -- the list goes on. Many of my 'once in a lifetime' experiences have made their way into my fiction in some way or another. Look for them.

It's safe to say I'm on a cyberpunk/LitRPG/technothriller binge at the moment. I am very interested in exploring artificial intelligence, quantum computing, virtual reality, human-android relations, addiction, mental disorders, neuronal dream worlds and advanced weaponry through my fiction.

**Also by Harmon Cooper**


Life is a Beautiful Thing Series (4 Books)

The Zero Patient Trilogy

Boy versus Self

Dear NSA

Tokyo Stirs

Zombie Lolita

Made in the USA
Middletown, DE
19 October 2016